THE BOBBSEY TWINS
AND THE COUNTY FAIR MYSTERY

The Bobbsey Twins and the County Fair Mystery

By

LAURA LEE HOPE

GROSSET & DUNLAP
A FILMWAYS COMPANY
Publishers • New York

The Bobbsey Twins and the County Fair Mystery

CONTENTS

CHAPTER I

THE CALLIOPE

"NAN! Flossie! Come quick!" Freddie Bobbsey called out as he ran into the house.

"What is it?" Nan asked her blond, blue-eyed brother, who was six.

"Come see what stopped at the corner. Hurry!" he added excitedly.

The screen door banged as Freddie darted back outside. His twin, Flossie, and twelve-year-old Nan were making sandwiches in the kitchen for their school picnic. They left their work and ran after him up the block.

"Oh, Freddie!" exclaimed Flossie. "A circus!"

At the corner, waiting for a stream of traffic to pass, was a strange and colorful caravan.

"It looks like *part* of a circus, anyway," agreed Nan.

1

Towed by a large truck were three flat trailers, each loaded with equipment for a merry-go-round. The first held various pieces of small baggage, tent poles, canvas tents, and parts of the smaller mechanisms for the merry-go-round. The two other trailers bore gilded seats and gaily painted wooden animals.

"Look!" Nan pointed enthusiastically. "There's a calliope!"

"What's a call-i-op-e?" Flossie asked.

"A piano that's run by steam," Nan explained. "See, it's on the last trailer."

Bringing up the rear of the procession was the steam piano. Even more brilliant than the animals, it was painted bright gold with red trim. At each end of the keyboard was a gilt cupid.

The three children ran to the curb to get a closer look at the musical machinery. Bert Bobbsey, Nan's dark-haired twin, stood there talking to a thin boy about his own age who sat at the rear of the third trailer, his feet dangling over the edge.

Freddie and the girls arrived in time to hear Bert ask, "Where are you going with that circus outfit?"

The boy smiled as he answered, "This isn't a circus. We're going to the Bolton County Fair."

"I've seen those fair grounds," Bert remarked. "They're not far from our Uncle Daniel Bobbsey's farm, Meadowbrook."

"Why don't you come over to the fair?" the boy suggested.

"We might at that!" Bert replied with a laugh.

"Well, look me up if you do. I'll be—"

A harsh voice interrupted the boy. "None of that now," it ordered threateningly. "Nobody's going to look you up."

The twins turned startled faces toward the truck and saw a huge, mean-looking man glaring down at them. His face was almost flat, and he had small shifty eyes and a nose like a hawk's beak. Nan shuddered and stepped back.

The boy did not finish his sentence but sat looking pale and unhappy. At this point the traffic let up, and the caravan moved on. It went very slowly and made a great deal of noise. At the rear of the calliope the twins saw painted in large letters:

FAGAN'S FAMOUS CALLIOPE

Bert saw the boy still watching them and waved to him. Nan and the younger twins did the same.

"Poor fellow!" exclaimed Bert.

"A mean man like that shouldn't be allowed to have a merry-go-round," Nan said firmly. "He doesn't want people to be happy."

"I'd still like to ride on it," said Flossie wistfully. "I saw a beautiful golden tiger I'd choose."

"I'd take the lion," asserted Freddie. "Do you think we can go to the fair, Bert?" he asked eagerly.

"I'd certainly like to. I'd like to hear a real steam calliope. It's great fun," replied his brother. "Maybe we can ask Dad tonight."

"Do you suppose that mean man was the Mr. Fagan in the sign?" asked Nan. "He has a wonderful merry-go-round even if he is horrible himself. I wish they had played the calliope while they were waiting."

"What's a calliope sound like?" asked Freddie.

"Well," said Bert smiling, "it goes um-pa-pa, um-pa-pa, toot, toot."

Nan joined her brother in the imitation while Freddie and Flossie clapped their hands excitedly.

Then, remembering why he had gone outside, Bert said, "I'm going to take Snap for a run around the block before the picnic." Snap was the Bobbseys' shaggy white dog.

"Oh goodness, we'll have to hurry, Flossie," declared Nan as they ran into the house. "It must be nearly time for the buses to pick us up."

Freddie, who had followed them into the kitchen, asked what he could do to help.

"You can pour the milk into the thermos bottles if you will, Freddie," Nan told him. "But be careful not to spill it on Dinah's clean floor."

Dinah Johnson was the plump, jolly colored woman who helped Mrs. Bobbsey with the housework. Her husband, Sam, drove a truck at the lumberyard which Mr. Bobbsey owned on the shore of Lake Metoka.

Freddie brought the four thermos bottles and set them carefully on the floor by the refrigerator. Then he opened the shiny white door and reached for two cartons of milk.

"I can take both at the same time," he murmured to himself as he tucked the first one under his arm. He reached for the second, but just then the carton under his arm began to slide.

"Catch it!" cried Freddie. "It's slipping."

Nan, who was cutting bread, turned quickly but was too late. Freddie had dropped the carton, which had opened. Milk was streaming over the floor. Flossie, running to help, slipped in the milk and fell!

Mrs. Bobbsey heard the sounds of distress and came hurrying into the kitchen. "Oh dear," said the twins' pretty mother. "Flossie, run up and change your clothes. I'll help Nan finish the

sandwiches. Freddie, get the mop quickly and wipe up this milk."

Just then Dinah came up from the basement. Seeing the confusion in the kitchen, she laughed

heartily. Soon everyone was laughing with her.

"Dinah, you're an angel!" exclaimed Nan. "We mess up your kitchen and your clean floor, and you just laugh."

Dinah shook her apron at them as though she

were shooing chickens. "You all just go on out of here," she said. "Your mother and I will see to the lunch."

The three children scampered away and Flossie ran upstairs to change into fresh clothes. When she came down, the lunch boxes and thermos bottles were on the porch. Bert was coming up the walk with Snap.

Freddie went to act as lookout and called presently that he could see the two buses coming down the street. There was a flurry of gathering sweaters, lunch boxes, and thermoses. Mrs. Bobbsey went outside to see the twins off.

The two buses drew up in front of the Bobbsey house, and Charlie Mason, Bert's special friend, leaned out of a window in the second bus. "There's room for all four of you here," he called. "Come on."

The twins climbed aboard, and the two buses started off. The children were glad to be with a group of their classmates again for one of the end-of-the-summer outings.

"What a glorious day for a picnic!" Nan remarked, as the buses left the town of Lakeport and rolled through the pleasant countryside. "I'm glad it rained last night so today would be fair."

"Speaking of fair," Bert said, "is anyone going to the Bolton County Fair?"

"Well, the Bobbseys are, I hope," Flossie piped up. "And I'm going to ride a golden tiger."

"Hot diggity!" cried Charlie. "Flossie on a tiger! That will be worth going to see!"

"It's on a merry-go-round," Freddie explained. "We saw one that was going to the fair."

"There were lions and elephants and beautiful golden thrones to ride on," Flossie went on, her golden curls bobbing and her blue eyes shining with excitement.

A stocky boy sitting in front of Bert turned around. He was Danny Rugg, who delighted in playing mean tricks on the other children, particularly the Bobbsey twins. "That's just kid stuff," Danny scoffed. "County fairs aren't anything much!"

"Well, you don't have to go, Danny," Bert remarked mildly and continued his conversation with Charlie Mason. "There was a boy just about our age sitting on the trailer."

"That would be keen!" Charlie exclaimed. "Imagine traveling around with a merry-go-round!"

"But there was a mean old man who wouldn't let the boy talk to us," Flossie put in.

"Do you suppose that man, Fagan, or whatever he's called, is the boy's father?" Nan asked her twin.

"I certainly hope not!" Bert replied. "Maybe we can find out at the fair."

"Oh my," said Charlie, "the Bobbseys are off on another mystery."

"I wouldn't say that," Bert protested.

"Well, every time you twins get curious about something, there's bound to be excitement!" his friend said.

The ride to the Pine Grove picnic grounds on the shore of Lake Metoka was a pretty one. The road wound through beautiful valleys and over rolling hills before it turned again toward the lake.

Finally the two buses parked on top of a grassy slope above the lake shore, and the children piled out. Carrying their picnic baskets, they ran over to the tables where the teachers and students were gathering.

Suddenly Bert looked at Nan. "Did you bring my camera from the bus?" he asked. When Nan shook her head he said, "I'll have to go back for it. I think I put it up on the rack."

When Bert reached the bus and climbed in, he saw Danny Rugg in the driver's seat.

"What are you doing? Playing driver?" Bert teased the bully.

Danny's face grew red. "It's none of your business, Bert Bobbsey!"

Bert grinned and went to the back of the bus

to get his camera. He found that it had slipped down and become wedged between the seat and the side of the bus, but he managed to free it. When he reached the front of the vehicle again, Danny was pulling on the emergency brake, then releasing it.

"Be careful!" Bert cried. "If you take that brake off, the bus will roll down the hill!"

"Don't tell me what to do!" Danny shouted furiously. He slipped out of the driver's seat and quickly left the bus. Bert followed.

As Bert stepped to the ground he felt the heavy vehicle begin to move. In another minute it had gained momentum and was rolling toward the water!

CHAPTER II

BERT ACCUSED

BERT began to run after the careening bus. As he did so, he noticed the figure of a boy disappear among the trees to the right of the picnic ground. "That's funny," he thought. "It looked like that boy on the merry-go-round trailer."

The commotion had brought the other children and the teachers running. The bus stopped as its front wheels became mired in the wet sand at the edge of the water.

Mr. Tetlow, the tall, gray-haired school principal, came up to where Bert and Danny were standing. "Which one of you released that brake?" he demanded. Both boys were pale and trembling. Neither one answered.

The principal looked stern. "Was it you, Danny?" he asked.

Danny scraped his toe in the sand, then mumbled, "No, sir. It was Bert Bobbsey!"

"It was not!" Bert cried indignantly.

"Which of you was the last to leave the bus?" Mr. Tetlow asked.

"I was, sir," Bert replied, "but I didn't release the brake!"

"I'm very disappointed in you, Bert," the principal said sadly. "We won't say any more about it now. I don't want to spoil the picnic."

In a few minutes the driver of the other bus had fastened a chain to the rear axle of the disabled vehicle. Several of the boys took off their shoes and socks and stepped into the water to help push. With a mighty heave the bus was pulled from the water to a safe parking place.

Seeing that the excitement was over, the children wandered back to the picnic grove and began to choose teams for various games.

Freddie ran up to Bert. "Remember you said you'd teach me to row?" he suggested. "You promised the next time we could get a boat you'd show me!"

Bert turned his eyes to the lake, which looked invitingly blue in the sunshine. "All right, Freddie," he agreed. "Does anyone else want to come along?"

"I'd love to," Nan declared.

"Me, too," Flossie cried.

Charlie said he would like nothing better, so

they all strolled down to the boathouse. Bert chose a boat with two rowing seats and two sets of oars.

Charlie found a paddle in the boathouse and said that he would steer from the back. Nan climbed forward into the bow of the boat while Bert seated both of the younger twins on one of the rowing seats.

"Each of you take an oar to begin," he told them. "It's easier that way because these oars are pretty heavy."

He took the other rowing seat, and Charlie stationed himself with the paddle in the stern. The boat glided out on the water.

"Dip your oars together," Bert directed. "Not too deep. Whoa! You nearly lost yours overboard, Flossie. It went too deep," her big brother told her. The oars dipped and skimmed the surface in jerks, splashing water into the boat.

"Oh! You're catching crabs," called Nan.

"Where?" cried Flossie, leaning over to scan the clear water. "I don't see any crabs."

"Nan means you're splashing because your oar hits the top of the water," explained Bert, laughing.

"Look out!" cried Nan, as Freddie's oar jerked out of his grip and, after balancing for a second on the boat's edge, went over with a soft splash. At that moment a motorboat sped past. Its backwash caught the oar and carried it farther away. The oar danced on the waves out of reach.

Bert pulled toward the oar with a few strong strokes. As the boat came up beside it, he leaned over to grab the runaway oar, but it bobbed teasingly away. Bert rowed after it, but as he leaned over, the boat rocked violently, nearly capsizing.

Flossie screamed, "Oh, Bert, please don't!" So Bert gave up the attempt.

"Let's go after the oar head on," suggested Nan. "I'll be able to reach it from the bow."

"That's a long reach," Bert objected. "I don't think you can do it."

"Let me try anyway," his twin urged, and Bert consented.

They came to where the oar lay on the surface of the sparkling water. Nan waited for the right moment to reach for it. Bert had pulled his oars into the boat and was half turned toward Nan when she said quietly, "Now."

Her head disappeared as she made a long grab for the oar. It slipped from her fingers, and she reached still farther. Suddenly Nan lost her balance. In another second she would have hit the water head first, but Bert leaped to grab her.

The small boat pitched dangerously from side to side as he pulled his twin back.

"I have it!" Nan gasped, as she regained her balance. The long oar was clutched in her hands and was restored, dripping, to a shame-faced Freddie.

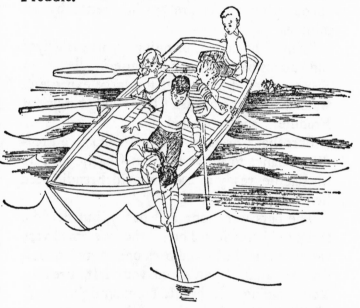

Flossie, a little upset by all the excitement, decided she would do no more rowing that day. She gave her oar to Freddie as well and slid over to share Charlie's seat in the stern.

"Now, Freddie, let's see how you can row by

yourself," Bert proposed as he took up his oars. "I'll give you some help for a while, and then you can take over entirely."

"Okay." Freddie nodded. He stiffened his small back and felt very proud. "Here we go." He pulled steadily on the oars, and Bert said encouragingly, "You're getting better by the minute.

"Now," he added, bringing in his oars, "you can row us back to the boathouse."

Nan glanced around at the large expanse of water before them. "Isn't it too long a row for Freddie?" she cautioned.

Bert shook his head. He wanted to give Freddie a chance to prove himself. Charlie took up his paddle, ready to use it should Freddie need help.

The oars were long and heavy, but Freddie stuck to his rowing. The boathouse seemed very far away, and he looked back once or twice. Bert directed him. "Harder on your left, Freddie. You're going in a circle. Now straight ahead. That's the boy!" he cheered.

On they went over the lake. Freddie was beginning to think that they would never arrive when Bert said suddenly, "All right, Freddie, I'll take over now. You did a powerful lot of rowing for the first time."

Bert brought the boat into the slip, and they all climbed ashore.

"That was a fine job, Freddie," Charlie congratulated him.

Nan patted her small brother on the back as she said, "I'm very proud to have such strong brothers. You're going to be just as good at everything as Bert is, Freddie."

Flossie remarked to her twin as they trudged up to the grove, "Now you can teach me to row some time when I'm bigger, Freddie—if I ever want to learn."

When they reached the grove they found the picnic baskets were being unpacked. Several teachers and children were scurrying around placing paper plates and cups at each place.

"That's good!" Freddie cried. "I'm hungry!"

"You're always hungry," Bert teased him.

"But I'm 'specially hungry today," Freddie declared. "I've had a lot of exercise!"

"What have you been doing, Freddie?" Miss Snell asked. She was one of the little boy's favorite teachers.

Freddie looked embarrassed. He wanted very much to tell Miss Snell about his feat of rowing, but he was afraid she would think he was boasting.

Flossie came to her twin's rescue. "Freddie

rowed our boat all the way to the boathouse from out in the middle of the lake!" she announced proudly.

"Why, that's wonderful. Congratulations!" Miss Snell said.

Bert and Charlie were seated farther down the table from Nan and the young twins. Bert told Charlie about finding Danny meddling with the brake in the bus.

"That's a dirty trick!" Charlie said indignantly. "And then he tells Mr. Tetlow that you did it. Danny is really a sneak!"

"Something funny happened," Bert went on. "When I ran after the bus, I thought I saw that boy I told you about—you know, the one on the trailer with the merry-go-round."

"What would he be doing around here?" Charlie asked in bewilderment.

"I don't know, but I'd like to scout around and see if I can find him."

"Okay, I'll go with you," Charlie agreed.

When the children had eaten all the fried chicken, potato salad, and chocolate cake that they could hold, they picked up the used plates and cups and deposited them in the trash cans.

Nan saw Bert and Charlie leave the table. "Where are you boys going?" she called.

"To see if we can find the merry-go-round,"

Bert told her. He explained about thinking he had seen the strange boy.

"I'd like to go, too," Nan said. "I'll get Freddie and Flossie. I promised Mother I'd look after them."

The five children walked out to the road and turned to the right. "Look!" Nan cried.

A short distance from where they stood in a wooded section of the road was the three-trailer caravan!

CHAPTER III

THE LONELY BOY

"THEY must be having trouble," Bert observed as the children looked down the road toward the caravan. Two men were peering helplessly into the open hood of the truck.

At that moment the little group heard the sound of running feet from the direction of the picnic grounds. Turning, they saw the other children hurrying toward them, followed by Mr. Tetlow and several of the teachers.

"What's going on?" the principal asked. "I don't want you children out on the highway. You might get hurt."

Nan pointed down the road to the stalled truck and trailers. "It's a merry-go-round," she explained. "It passed our house this morning on the way to the Bolton County Fair."

"Please, may we go down to see it?" Flossie begged.

20

"Well, all right," Mr. Tetlow replied, "but be careful and stay at the side of the road. I'll follow you."

The children were excited to find such a spectacular caravan and ran to get a close look at the calliope and the painted animals.

"There's my golden tiger," squealed Flossie, pointing her finger at the wooden animal glittering in the sun.

"And here's my lion," Freddie shouted.

The other children ran around the trailer, each choosing a steed which he or she would like to ride on the merry-go-round.

"It looks strange on the highway away from the rest of the circus," Mr. Tetlow observed with a chuckle.

Bert told him that when the Bobbseys had seen the caravan passing their house, they had talked to a pale, sad-looking boy sitting on the end of the last trailer.

"I wonder where he is now," Nan mused. "There was the most awful man—"

Before she could finish her sentence a harsh voice bellowed, "Hey, you! Get away from that trailer! I got too many troubles without a pack of nosy kids underfoot. Scram, all of you!"

The twins recognized the voice and figure coming rapidly toward the startled children.

Nan turned to Mr. Tetlow. "That's the man," she whispered.

The fellow picked up a stick by the roadside as he advanced, and the children fled to stand near Mr. Tetlow and the teachers.

The principal said, "There's no need for that stick. I'm sorry if the children are bothering you, but after all, you can't blame them for being excited about a merry-go-round."

The man had not seen Mr. Tetlow until the latter spoke. He now tossed away the stick and changed his tone to a whine.

"Sorry, sir. I've had nothing but trouble on this trip. The truck is old and broken down, the weather's been bad—seems like everything happens to me." He sighed heavily.

"That's too bad," Mr. Tetlow said. "But the children were doing no harm. Where are you taking this circus apparatus, may I ask?"

The man replied, "It has nothing to do with a circus. This is Fagan's Famous Calliope," he bragged. "I'm Fagan, and I'm taking this to the Bolton County Fair."

Just then a man came back to say, "I'm sorry, Ben, but the driver says he'll have to take the truck to a town up the road a ways for repair. He's got it started, but he doesn't want to pull a load until the motor's fixed. The trailers and calliope will have to stay here until he can get back."

Ben Fagan turned in a rage and shouted such a flow of angry words that his listeners drew hastily away from him.

The other man interrupted impatiently, "That's the way it is, Ben. I'll go along with the truck now and see that everything gets fixed up."

"All right, Bates," said Ben Fagan. "But make it quick!"

With that the man called Bates hurried away, and presently the truck went groaning and banging down the highway.

Mr. Fagan fumed, but he was helpless. "I'm losing money by the minute," he growled. "If we were stuck in a town, I could at least pick up a few dollars by playing the calliope and passing the hat, but here on a back country road—"

Mr. Tetlow looked at the golden pipes of the steam piano shining in the sun. Then he made a suggestion. "Mr. Fagan, if you can get steam up, how about playing for the children? I'll give you five dollars if you'll play until the truck returns."

The children clapped their hands in joy and then waited breathlessly for Mr. Fagan's reply.

The cold little eyes in Ben Fagan's flat face glistened as he looked at Mr. Tetlow. Then he said cautiously, "We'll play for an hour for five dollars."

Mr. Tetlow smiled slightly. "I can see you drive a hard bargain, Mr. Fagan," he commented. "All right, but if the truck returns in less than an hour you must stick to your agreement."

The man nodded curtly and then turned to call out in his coarse voice, "Billy! Billy! Get a move on there! You're going to play some tunes for these folks."

From under the tent pile in the second trailer the boy's head appeared. He looked at the children, who were still staring eagerly at the cavalcade on the edge of the road. Then he caught sight of Bert and Nan, and his thin face broke into a wide smile.

"Billy," Ben Fagan said as he advanced toward the trailer, "get out of there and help me stoke the boiler."

Billy jumped off the trailer and ran to climb aboard the platform holding the calliope. He and Fagan fed wood into a small stove connected to the boiler. The machinery presently began to sputter, and a few minutes later odd tooting music issued from the calliope while steam poured from the pipes.

The children shrieked in delight and began to

caper about. Square dances were formed by the teachers, and the green lawn at the grove entrance was a colorful scene. Bert, Charlie, and Nan walked toward the calliope with the idea of talking to Billy. They sat down on the grass by the roadside to watch him at the keyboard surrounded by the horseshoe of pipe whistles. He seemed to know all the music by heart, and one tune after another wheezed forth from the calliope's pipes.

Nan, who played the piano, watched with great interest. She whispered to Bert, "Do you think I could play that queer instrument? The keyboard looks like the piano."

Bert answered loyally, "I'll bet you could. Shall I ask Billy to give you a try?"

"Oh, yes!" Nan exclaimed. "I'd love to."

Bert went to the side nearest Billy and asked if his sister might have a try at the calliope. He added, "She plays the piano very well."

The boy smiled and motioned to Nan to sit beside him on the bench. He took off a pair of white gloves and handed them to Nan, explaining, "These brass keys get hot from all the steam, so you have to wear these asbestos gloves to protect your fingers. It's not like playing the piano, you know." He smiled. "The keys are pretty stiff so you really have to bear down on them."

Nan nodded and put on the gloves. At first she stumbled a little over the keys, but soon she was playing some lively popular tunes.

All at once the ugly face of Ben Fagan appeared around the side of the calliope. He was perspiring freely, and the soot and ashes from the stove were smeared over his face, hands, and clothes. His unpleasant voice thundered in Nan's ear. "What are you doing there? Get down and don't come back! You'll ruin my calliope!"

Nan drew herself up and looked at the dirty, flat face with its beady eyes. "I haven't hurt your calliope, Mr. Fagan," she said. "I've taken piano lessons for several years, and I just wanted to try—"

Billy said nothing, but Nan could see that he was embarrassed by Ben Fagan's rudeness. She hopped down and joined Bert and Charlie, who had watched the scene indignantly.

Mr. Fagan turned to them. "Why don't you go away and leave the boy alone? He has work to do and hasn't time for you," he said crossly.

Bert turned to wave at Billy, who stared wistfully after them as the three walked away. It was growing very warm, and Nan noticed that the sun shone directly down on the boy and the steam from the whistling pipes blew into his face.

"Poor fellow!" Nan sighed. "What a life he must have with that man!"

"I wonder if he's any relation to Fagan," mused Bert. "I can't see why he stays with that grouch if he isn't. I think I'll get a lemonade and take it to him."

He hurried to the picnic supplies while Nan and Charlie went over to the dancers. Even the teachers had joined in the fun, leading the children in merry circles. The music went on and on.

Bert brought the cold drink and put it on the bench beside Billy. He had to watch his chance while Ben Fagan was busy at the boiler, for he feared the man would not let the boy stop long enough to enjoy his drink.

The sun grew hotter and hotter, and at last the dances came to an end even though the calliope continued. The children, hot and thirsty, lined up for lemonade. Bert was about to take another cold drink to Billy when Mr. Tetlow came to the entrance of the grove and gave a shrill whistle for everyone's attention.

"Hear ye! Hear ye! The ice cream is in danger of melting. Will the orchestra please come and join us at the table?"

Everyone clapped and cheered as Billy came shyly away from the calliope and across to the grove. Bert and Charlie made room for him on the bench between them. Bert suggested, "Tell me your full name, Billy. I want to introduce you to the others."

The boy answered quietly, "I'm Billy Fagan."

"Oh!" Nan exclaimed. "Is that—that man your father?"

Billy smiled at her. Then he said slowly, "Well, not exactly. You see, he—"

Billy stopped abruptly, and Bert saw that Ben Fagan had just seated himself directly opposite and was glaring at them.

Bert stood up and announced, "Ladies and gentlemen!"

Giggles greeted this formal address. He continued, "This is Billy Fagan, everybody. He's the one who played all the music for us."

Bert sat down, and three cheers went up for Billy Fagan. Nan looked at Mr. Fagan, thinking that now, surely, he would be smiling. Instead, his hard little eyes were angry and his mouth uglier than ever.

Billy was plainly embarrassed and began to eat his ice cream rapidly.

Nan, who had been watching Billy, came presently to bring him another dish of ice cream and more cake. "Our Dinah made this cake," she told him. "You're the only one here who's been working, so you deserve the lion's share."

Mr. Tetlow now seated himself by Ben Fagan. He leaned across the table to speak to Billy. "You play that calliope very easily, Billy, and you really do a fine job. How long did it take you to learn to play?"

Billy flushed with pleasure at the compliment. He hesitated, then answered with a short laugh, "Well, not very long. You see—"

Ben Fagan interrupted him. "Never mind about that," he told the boy roughly. "These people aren't interested in your life story."

Nan started to protest, but she saw that Ben Fagan was determined to keep the boy quiet. Why, she wondered, was Mr. Fagan afraid to let Billy make any friends?

CHAPTER IV

A MISSING CAMERA

IN VAIN Bert and Charlie tried to find out more about Billy, but Ben Fagan put an end to conversation between the boys.

They were startled when the man suddenly jumped to his feet, jarring the table violently as he did so. "Let's get a move on, Billy," he commanded abruptly.

"But the boy hasn't finished his dessert," Miss Snell protested.

Ben Fagan seemed flustered for a moment by the unexpected intervention. Mr. Tetlow took advantage of the man's hesitation and said firmly, "Sit down, Billy, and finish your ice cream and cake. I'm sure Mr. Fagan can wait." He put a hand on the boy's shoulder and gently pushed him to the seat.

31

Billy looked up fearfully at Ben Fagan, who shrugged indifferently. "Go ahead and eat," he told the boy. "But make it snappy."

Billy obeyed, casting a thankful glance toward Mr. Tetlow.

"We've got to get out of here soon," Fagan went on. "Time's going, and the truck'll be back." He turned to Mr. Tetlow. "What about the money?" he demanded. "I guess you got your five dollars' worth."

Mr. Tetlow took a five-dollar bill from his wallet. "Indeed we did," he exclaimed, "thanks to Billy."

Ben Fagan almost snatched the bill from the principal in his eagerness to get the money. He muttered gruffly, "That's all he's good for, the lazy boy." Then the man started off through the grove, roaring at Billy to hurry along.

"Well!" exclaimed Nan. "I'm glad he isn't your *real* father, Billy."

The boy nodded sadly. "No. Ben Fagan adopted me when I was very young."

"Won't you have time for a game of ball?" Bert asked him in order to change the subject. "He'll call you when the truck comes."

Billy shook his head. "I wouldn't know how. I've never played games," he told the astonished boys. "Anyway, Ben'll be very mad if I don't go now. I'll be in for a lot of trouble later if I don't obey him."

"He's not very nice to you, is he?" Freddie asked.

"I think he's an awful man," Flossie added. "He's cross as an old bear."

Ben Fagan's bellow came through the grove as if to prove her words. "Billy! Get out here! The truck's coming." As the boy said good-by to Mr. Tetlow and Miss Snell, he thanked them for the cake and ice cream. "It's the nicest day I ever had," he told them shyly.

The twins and Charlie walked up to the road with the boy. When they reached the highway, Mr. Fagan was in the first trailer just closing the lid of one of the trunks. He ordered Billy to get aboard at once. They could see the truck coming back down the road at great speed.

Billy held out his hand to Bert. "Good-by, and thanks for everything," he said. Then in a low voice he added, "Try to get to the fair if you can. I'd like to see you again."

They all shook his hand, and Bert answered in the same quiet tone, "We'll see what we can do about that."

"I'll ask Daddy tonight if we can come to the fair," Freddie piped up.

Mr. Fagan heard him. "Billy! Get up there on

that trailer, and don't dawdle about it." The man sounded as though he meant business, so the twins waved good-by to Billy. The truck attached its load and soon went rumbling off up the highway.

"I hope we're not too late to get in the ball game!" Charlie said as the children started back.

He and Bert dashed at top speed toward the field. The younger twins were whisked off to enter a three-legged race. Nan, left alone, wondered where all her girl friends were.

Grace Lavine's voice hailed her, "Nan Bobbsey! We were looking for you. Come over here and see the archery set Phyllis brought."

Nan hurried to the far side of the grove where there was a group of girls. They had set the target on the stump of a large tree and were standing back some ten or twelve yards from it. Phyllis held a large, graceful bow and a quiver of long arrows.

"We came 'way over here to practice where no one would be walking," she told Nan.

"What a beautiful set!" Nan exclaimed. "That bull's-eye is certainly a tempting target."

"We'll take turns," explained Phyllis. "There are six arrows so we'll each have six tries."

At first the arrows fell far short of the target,

but soon the girls learned to gauge the distance more expertly. On Nan's fifth try one arrow went to the very rim of the bull's-eye, and there was a shout from the girls.

"Did it hit the mark? Good for you, Nan!"

"No," she replied truthfully. "But this one will!"

She took aim and stood poised, trying to send the last one in a perfect line to the center of the target. The arrow left her fingers just as Flossie's voice rang out, and Nan saw her little sister running toward her, directly in line with the target!

"Flossie, look out!" Nan shrieked and shut her eyes, expecting to hear the child's agonized cry. There was no sound but the thud of the arrow. Nan opened her eyes and saw Flossie lying on the ground. She dashed to her small sister's side, as the other girls ran to help her.

To her amazement and joy, Flossie rolled over before Nan could reach her. The little girl scrambled to her feet.

"I tripped over that old thing," she complained, kicking at a gnarled tree root almost covered by long grass.

"Thank goodness!" Nan said, hugging her tight. "That old root saved you from being hit by my arrow!"

At that moment there was a shout from Phyllis Drake. "Nan! Your last arrow went right in the middle of the bull's-eye!"

As the girls crowded around the target to see, Nan did not feel as triumphant as she otherwise would have. She was too thankful that the arrow had missed Flossie.

"Now that I've hit the bull's-eye I think I'll stop," she said. "I've had enough for today."

"Oh, Nan," Flossie cried, "don't stop. I'd like to shoot an arrow, too!"

"I'm afraid you're not strong enough, honey," Nan said. "But when you get bigger Bert and I will show you how."

Phyllis Drake overheard the conversation. "There's a lightweight bow here, Nan, that my little sister uses. Maybe Flossie could try that," she suggested.

Flossie's eyes shone. "Yes, Nan, please let me! Just once!"

When Nan consented, Flossie took the proffered small bow and arrow. Holding the bow tight in her left hand, she pulled back the arrow and let it fly. It hit one corner of the target!

Flossie clapped her hands and squealed, "I hit it! I hit it!"

"That was very good," Nan praised her little sister. "Now come on, let's go watch Bert play ball."

But when the two girls reached the picnic spot they found that the ball game was over. Excitedly Flossie told Bert about the archery match. "Nan shot an arrow right in the bull's-eye," she exclaimed. "And I hit the target!"

"That's great!" Bert said. "I think I should have a picture of you two shooting arrows!"

"Oh, Bert, *would* you take our pictures?" Flossie said excitedly.

"Sure. I'll get my camera." The boy walked over to the picnic table where he thought he had left it.

The camera was not there. Bert looked puzzled for a moment, then his face cleared. "I know!" he cried. "I had it with me when we went out to the road. I put it down on a tree stump when I took the lemonade to Billy."

He ran out to the road. When he did not return in a few minutes, Nan followed. She saw Bert rummaging in the bushes by the roadside.

"What's the matter? Can't you find it?" she asked.

"No. And I'm sure I left it here."

"You don't suppose Danny Rugg took your camera for a joke?" Nan asked.

"He may be sneaky," Bert admitted, "but I don't think he'd do a thing like that."

"Maybe somebody picked it up by mistake," Nan ventured. "Let's report it to Mr. Tetlow, and he can make an announcement."

As the older twins approached the picnic area again, Flossie ran up. "Where's the camera, Bert?" she asked. Her eyes opened wide when Bert explained that it had disappeared.

When the Bobbseys told Mr. Tetlow of the loss

he quickly picked up a small megaphone. "Bert Bobbsey's camera is missing," he called. "Has anyone seen it?"

Picnic baskets and belongings which had been gathered together in preparation for departure were carefully searched, but no trace of the camera was found.

Suddenly Freddie piped up, "I'll bet I know who took it!"

Mr. Tetlow looked stern. "Be careful, Freddie. You must never accuse anyone of stealing unless you have proof."

Freddie looked abashed for a moment, then he spoke up stoutly, "I think that mean old Mr. Fagan took it!"

CHAPTER V

THE RUNAWAY

WHEN Freddie accused Ben Fagan of taking Bert's camera Nan looked thoughtful. "He could have, you know," she said. "He didn't come to the picnic table for his ice cream until after all of us were there. He had a chance to pick it up and hide it after the rest of us left the trailer."

"That's another reason why we should go to the fair," Flossie put in. "If that awful man does have Bert's camera, we'll get it back."

Mr. Tetlow announced that the buses were waiting to go home, so the children piled on. The ride back to Lakeport seemed very short as the tired but happy picnickers sang song after song.

At one point, Bert stopped singing. His mind was filled with thoughts of what Mr. Tetlow would do about the bus incident. The boy hoped he could convince the principal that he had not been the culprit.

When the bus pulled up at the Bobbsey home, the twins said good-by to their friends and hopped off. Mr. and Mrs. Bobbsey were waiting to welcome the four children.

In the next few minutes everyone talked at once, relating the exciting events of the picnic and telling about the loss of Bert's camera.

Flossie was just describing her archery try when Dinah appeared at the door. She beckoned mysteriously.

"What is it, Dinah?" Nan asked.

"There's something mighty queer going on," the cook replied. "I think you all had better come with me."

Dinah quickly led the way to the sun porch, gesturing for them to be quiet. At the doorway she stopped and pointed dramatically to the big couch at the far end of the porch.

A queer groaning and growling issued from under the couch, and the tip of a brown fur tail came into view.

"See that?" Dinah whispered, her eyes twinkling. "There's two wild animals under there in a fight to the finish!"

"You're teasing us, Dinah," Freddie cried. "That's Snap!"

"Snap can't get under that couch," Dinah replied. "He's too big now. And besides, his tail's white!" she added triumphantly.

Flossie's eyes grew large. "Do you really think it's a wild animal?" she asked fearfully.

"Of course not, honey," Nan said.

A sharp bark sent Bert racing across the sun porch. "We'll soon find out," he called. Getting down on his hands and knees, he peered beneath the sofa.

"It *is* Snap!" he cried. "He's caught under here!"

Mr. Bobbsey helped Bert lift the heavy piece of furniture, and out crawled Snap. His tail was between his legs and he looked very much ashamed of himself. He went over to Bert and licked the boy's hand.

"Where's that other animal?" Dinah asked warily as she came across the room. "That wasn't Snap's tail!"

Freddie threw himself on the floor, reached under the sofa, and pulled out a furry object. *It was Mrs. Bobbsey's furpiece!*

"So *that's* the wild animal!" The twins' mother laughed as she hastily rescued her fur. "I'm glad it's not damaged. I remember now, I left it on a chair in my bedroom when I was straightening out my closet yesterday. Evidently Snap couldn't resist it!"

Nan looked puzzled. "Snap must think he's a puppy again," she said. "He hasn't done anything like that for a long time."

Flossie put her arms around the dog's neck. "I think he was lonesome because he couldn't go to the picnic with us. He took the fur under there for company!"

Snap only wagged his tail.

"He certainly is glad to see us," Bert agreed. "Come on, boy. I'll take you for a run around the block."

As Nan and Flossie carried the picnic things into the kitchen, they found Dinah chuckling over Snap and the furpiece. When Nan started to rinse the thermos bottles, the kind-hearted woman sent her away, saying she would take care of them.

"You children better go get cleaned up for supper," she remarked. "It'll soon be ready."

As the meal progressed the talk turned to Bert's missing camera. "Are you sure one of the other children didn't pick it up by mistake?" Mr. Bobbsey asked.

"Oh yes, Dad," Nan spoke up. "Mr. Tetlow announced that it was missing, and no one knew anything about it!"

"Not even Danny Rugg," Flossie added.

"I still think it was that mean old man," Freddie stated positively.

Mr. Bobbsey nodded slowly. "Perhaps you're right, Freddie," he observed. "Ben Fagan seems the most likely suspect. He evidently had a good opportunity. Of course we have no proof," he added quickly.

"Let's go to the Bolton County Fair and maybe we can find the camera," urged Freddie eagerly.

"Yes, let's!" Flossie cried.

"How about that, Dad?" said Bert eagerly. "We can stay at Meadowbrook. It's very close to the fair grounds."

"We're pretty good detectives, Daddy. Maybe we could solve the mystery," Nan added. "Anyway, it would be lots of fun to go to a big county fair."

Mr. Bobbsey laughed as he answered, "That's a very good reason for going, Nan. I think the trip would be a pleasant one. And if we can find Bert's camera, it will be profitable, too."

Mrs. Bobbsey suggested that her husband call his brother Daniel before they made plans, adding, "Remember, this is a very busy time on the farm, and it might not be convenient for Daniel to have guests."

After dinner Mr. Bobbsey put in a call to Meadowbrook and came from the telephone with a broad smile.

"Aunt Sarah, Uncle Daniel, and Harry are all

delighted to have us," he said. "My brother is exhibiting some of his sheep at the fair so he'll be going over every day. They want us to stay the entire week, but I think four or five days are all I can spare from my lumberyard."

"Nifty!" Bert exclaimed. The younger twins squealed in delight.

Two days later the Bobbseys were on their way to Meadowbrook. It was a beautiful morning as the family station wagon with its happy occupants traveled along the highway. It grew very hot, and they were glad to find a shaded outdoor restaurant by the roadside.

There were tables under the trees by a cool brook which bubbled refreshingly over pretty stones. As the Bobbseys turned into the parking lot Freddie cried, pointing to a van parked nearby:

"Wow! That's a beauty!"

The graceful head and neck of a horse protruded from a small window at the back. The animal looked at the Bobbseys with great interest. Freddie jumped out of the car and ran over to the van.

"Look at his forehead. He has a white star on it!"

"Oh, yes," agreed Flossie who had followed her twin from the station wagon. "And his coat is so black it makes the star stand out even more!"

Freddie stood on tiptoe, trying to pat the horse's nose, which was as low as the friendly animal could reach toward the little boy.

At that moment the driver of the van came out of the restaurant. "Would you like to give White Star a lump of sugar?" he asked Freddie. The man reached into his pocket and pulled some out.

"Oh, would I!" Freddie beamed with pleasure as the man lifted him level with the horse's head.

Freddie held the lump of sugar flat on the palm of his hand. White Star took it gently. "He certainly is a pretty horse," Freddie declared.

The driver answered proudly, "White Star is the finest horse in the Manley stables."

"I wish we had a horse," Freddie said longingly, as he watched the handsome black creature munch the sugar.

"Maybe you will some day." The driver laughed as he set the little boy down. He patted the horse's black nose. "We're sure the Star here is going to win the big race."

Bert, who had been standing near, asked, "Where is he running, sir?"

"We're on our way to the Bolton County Fair."

"So are we!" cried Freddie. "Goody! I can see the race!"

Freddie held the lump of sugar flat on the palm of his hand

"You certainly can then," the man replied. "They have races every day, and the final one for the winners will be on the last day."

"White Star just has to win!" breathed Freddie. "He *has* to."

"Well, he has your blessing anyway." The driver laughed as he climbed into the driver's seat. "He'll do his best."

"I'll come to see him at the fair," called Freddie as the van moved away. The driver waved and smiled.

Bert, Freddie, and Flossie went to join the others, who were seated at a table under the trees. "Isn't this perfect?" said Nan dreamily. "I could stay here all day listening to that little brook."

Freddie was still thinking about White Star. "His coat is as black and shiny as can be," he said. "And he's going to win the race at the county fair."

"Now that the race is settled," Mr. Bobbsey said, laughing, "what will you all have to eat? We have plenty of time, so order whatever you like."

Bert studied the menu, but Freddie put a lump of sugar flat on the palm of his hand. He tried to pick it up with his lips as White Star had done.

"See," he said to Flossie. "White Star didn't touch his teeth to my hand at all. It's awfully hard to eat sugar that way."

"What will you have besides sugar, Freddie?" Mr. Bobbsey asked him. "It's quite a while before suppertime," he warned.

"I'll have the roast beef sandwich," Bert decided, "and a big glass of milk."

Freddie usually tried to be as much like his big brother as possible so he said, "That's for me, too."

The Bobbseys found they were hungrier than they had realized, and all enjoyed the luncheon very much.

As they lingered over dessert, listening to the bubbling brook and the bird songs, Nan said, "See that poor boy walking on the highway in this heat! I wonder why he doesn't wait in the shade 'til it's cooler."

The others turned and saw a boy about Bert's age trudging along the sun-baked road. He seemed to be in a hurry.

Suddenly Bert gave an exclamation and jumped to his feet. "That's Billy Fagan!" he cried out. He stood up and called the boy's name.

Billy seemed delighted and surprised to see him. He came quickly to the Bobbseys' table, but when Bert introduced him to Mr. and Mrs. Bobbsey and Mr. Bobbsey offered him a chair, he shook his head.

"I can't stop," he said, looking very tired and worried. "I'm running away! I've stood all I can from Ben Fagan!"

CHAPTER VI

THE TRAVELING MUSICIANS

MR. BOBBSEY looked at Billy's exhausted face, then led the boy gently to a chair.

"Look, Billy, you must take a little time to rest. We're your friends, and we want to help you."

He signaled a waiter and gave him an order quietly while the twins told Billy how glad they were to see him again.

"I don't blame you for leaving," Bert told him. "I wonder that you didn't run away long ago."

Mr. Bobbsey put a hand on Billy's shoulder for a moment as he asked, "When did you leave the fair grounds?"

"This morning before sunrise," Billy answered wearily. "I decided during the night that I just couldn't take any more."

Mrs. Bobbsey said quickly, "What you need is food, Billy, and here it comes."

The waiter put down a heaping plate of meat and vegetables and a large glass of milk.

Mr. Bobbsey told the tired boy, "Now, no talking until you put most of that under your belt."

While Billy ate, the twins told him the story about Dinah, Snap and the furpiece, which made him laugh, and some color came back into his face. He seemed to enjoy his lunch more after that.

"Dinah must be great fun," he remarked with a chuckle. He had cleaned his plate, and seemed a little surprised at his own appetite.

"Now," Mrs. Bobbsey said, "we'll let you tell your story."

"First of all," Mr. Bobbsey added, "has Ben Fagan proof that he adopted you legally?"

Billy looked uncertain. Then he answered, "I don't know, because I never asked him, Mr. Bobbsey."

"Can you remember anything about your life before Ben Fagan adopted you, Billy? Do you know how old you were then?" Mr. Bobbsey went on.

"Yes, sir. I must have been about six. I don't remember my mother and father. I lived with a man I called Alec, who told me my parents were dead. He had been their friend, and he took me in after they were killed in an accident. He had a little house filled with all kinds of musical instruments, and he could play them all. He made me a little fiddle and taught me to play it. He taught me to read, too, so I know I must have been about six when we went to the city."

"What city was that?" asked Mr. Bobbsey.

"I'm not quite sure. Alec's house was in a little village on the shore down South, and the city was quite a distance from there. We walked part of the way, and then someone picked us up in a car. We took my fiddle and Alec had his accordion. He said we could make more money playing in a big town."

"Where is your fiddle now?" Flossie asked.

"I outgrew it a few years ago," Billy told her, smiling. "I wish I had it now to give to you."

"Don't interrupt, Flossie dear," Mrs. Bobbsey said gently.

"We went to the busiest street corner," Billy went on. "We played there for two or three hours and collected enough money for a good dinner. There was a restaurant nearby, so we went in and Alec bought us more food than we'd had for a long time.

"After that we went out again and started to play. All at once a car came roaring up the street and jumped the curb. It knocked Alec down, but the driver went on without stopping. I tried to lift Alec, but he was too heavy. A crowd came and pushed me aside. Then police cars drove up, and they took Alec away in an ambulance. No one paid any attention to me, though. I had Alec's accordion, my fiddle, and the little bag which I am carrying now."

Billy pointed to the small satchel at his feet. The Bobbseys waited expectantly as he continued.

"I went into the restaurant, but the people were all busy and told me to go away. Instead I stood in the corner of the room and played on my fiddle. The customers all clapped and wanted more, so the manager let me stay. I played until almost everyone had gone and the manager told me to go home. I said I had no place to go and tried to tell him about Alec, but he said I should notify the police.

"Just then a man who had been sitting at a table came over and said he'd take me to the police station. I didn't like his looks, but there was nothing for me to do but go with him."

"And who was that man?" Mr. Bobbsey asked.

"Ben Fagan," Billy explained. "He asked me if I could sing and dance as well as play the fiddle. I said I thought I could. Ben swears he took me to the police station to find out who I was and what happened to Alec, but I have no recollection of anything more that night. I guess I was pretty tired and sleepy by that time."

"Of course you were, poor boy!" Mrs. Bobbsey exclaimed. "I don't understand why someone didn't take care of you!"

"If Fagan did take you to the police station as a lost child," Mr. Bobbsey observed, "they would have held you there until they could find out the truth."

"I know. That's why I don't think he did take me there. I figure Alec must have died from the accident or he would have found me somehow. I'm not sure that I ever knew Alec's full name. If I did I've forgotten it."

"What happened then?" Freddie asked, eager for the rest of the story.

"Mr. Fagan was trying to organize a show to take on the road. We rehearsed in an old barn somewhere outside the town. I had to learn to sing and dance while I played the fiddle.

"The show failed, and then Mr. Bates, Ben Fagan's present partner, came along. He knew of a circus that was selling out, so he and Ben bought the merry-go-round and calliope. The man who played for the dancers taught me to play the calliope. He had played one on a showboat on the Mississippi River years ago. He called it a cally-ope," Billy remembered, smiling.

"What about school?" Bert asked.

"I went for a few weeks in a little town called Allenton one spring when I was about nine. Ben was having the merry-go-round and the calliope fixed up there. He promised the truant officer that he would teach me himself every day while we were traveling with the merry-go-round. Of course he never did."

"What a meanie!" exclaimed Freddie.

"One of the ladies in the show used to have me read to her a lot of the time, so I had good practice in that. I like to read, and sometimes when we were going to be in a town for a while I went to the library to find books about the world. Mr. Bates was always pretty nice to me, when Ben Fagan wasn't around."

Nan's attention had been caught by a car which was traveling very slowly along the highway. Two men in it were scanning the area about the restaurant. She recognized with a start that one of the men was Ben Fagan. He must have caught sight of Billy, for at that moment the car swerved quickly into the parking lot.

"He's here!" Nan said in a loud whisper. "Mr. Fagan and another man are coming this way!"

The two men got out of the car and walked rapidly toward the table where Billy and the Bobbseys were sitting.

Bert looked at Billy's despairing face and said in a low voice, "Cheer up, we're on your side."

It was obvious that Ben Fagan was in a rage. He strode to Billy's side and grabbed his arm as though he would jerk the boy from his chair.

Mr. Bobbsey rose and said in a commanding voice, "Just a moment, Mr. Fagan. Billy is our guest. I suggest that if you have something to say to him you do it politely."

The other man, standing behind, cautioned, "Take it easy, Fagan."

"I'll have you arrested for scheming with this ungrateful scamp! You helped him run off like a sneak!" Ben Fagan sputtered.

Mr. Bobbsey interrupted him. "What proof have you that Billy is your adopted son?"

A triumphant smile came over Ben Fagan's ugly face as he took a folded, worn paper from his pocket and thrust it into Mr. Bobbsey's hand. While the twins' father studied it, Bert looked at Mr. Fagan's companion. The man's face seemed slightly familiar, and as he saw Bert watching him he smiled and said:

"Aren't you the twins that come to visit at Meadowbrook Farm? I live down the road from there, and I've seen you with Harry."

"He's our cousin, and we're going to visit him now," Freddie explained. "And we're going to the fair, too," he added.

"Well then, look me up," the man said. "I'm Detective Sheldon of the local force, and I'm stationed at the fair."

Mr. Bobbsey handed the paper back to Ben

Fagan. "Well, whether or not you are Billy's legal guardian," he said slowly, "I intend to see that he gets better treatment. The proper authorities will be notified, and Billy will be taken away from you if you continue to overwork and mistreat the boy."

Ben Fagan's flat face was a mixture of anger and fear. His voice took on a whining tone as he said, "Oh, now, Mr. Bobbsey, you can't believe all those lies the boy's been telling you. He's been treated like my own son all these years. Come on, Billy. We're wasting time over this foolishness. I'll forgive you this time."

Billy resisted his guardian's helping hand as he rose from the chair. He looked at Mr. Bobbsey, who turned to the detective and said sternly, "You're on duty at the fair grounds?"

"Yes, I am. I came with Mr. Fagan to look for his runaway son, but according to what you say, maybe the boy had good reason for leaving."

Mr. Bobbsey nodded and observed, "I'm quite sure he did. Will you please keep an eye on Billy and see that he doesn't play that calliope continuously all day? We'll be at the fair for a few days, and I intend to check further into this matter."

He turned to Billy and put his hand on the boy's shoulder. "We'll be seeing you often."

The twins, who had been standing silent during this exchange, now wished Billy good luck with all their hearts. He looked back and waved as he left in the car with Ben Fagan and the fair-grounds detective.

The Bobbseys soon were on their way, too. Suddenly Flossie exclaimed, "Daddy! You never asked Mr. Fagan about Bert's camera!"

"So I didn't, dear," her father responded. "I forgot all about it."

"Maybe you can ask him tomorrow," Mrs. Bobbsey suggested.

When the family arrived at Meadowbrook they were joyfully greeted by their relatives, Aunt Sarah, Uncle Daniel, and Cousin Harry.

"You're just in time to help feed the animals," declared Uncle Daniel.

Nan and Flossie put out milk for the fluffy little kittens while Freddie went straight to the barn to watch his uncle fill the feed boxes for the sturdy gray horses. Bert and Harry, while catching up on news, stopped at the pond to try their luck at catching bullfrogs.

Later, after the delicious farm supper, Freddie wandered out to the pond. "Maybe I can catch a frog," he thought. "I'll surprise Bert and Harry."

A huge bullfrog was seated on a water lily

pad about a yard from shore. Freddie crept
softly up to the pond, then reached out quickly
to grab the frog. As he did, his foot slipped on
the muddy edge and down he went head first into
the murky water among the lilies!

CHAPTER VII

WHITE STAR'S DANGER

A FEW minutes after Freddie left the house, Bert and Harry decided to race to the pond. Bert was ahead and had reached the turn in the path when he heard a tremendous splash.

"Wow!" he shouted. "That must have been the great-grand-daddy frog of them all!"

When the boys drew up at the edge of the pond they were surprised to see many small ripples circling in wide rings on the dark water. As they stood wondering, Bert caught sight of a small hand reaching out from the center of the whirlpool.

"Jeepers!" he cried. "There's someone in there!"

He knelt down, and as he leaned out to grab the hand he saw Freddie's familiar yellow head rising to the surface.

"Freddie!" Bert gasped.

The little boy shook the water from his ears as he was helped out, and said with chattering teeth, "I f-fell in, Bert. My foot got tangled in something, and I c-couldn't get loose."

Harry peered into the water and exclaimed, "Golly! Those water lily roots are thick down there. That's dangerous! What if we hadn't heard that splash?"

"Never mind," said Bert quickly. He saw that his little brother was shaking with chill, so he led him toward the house.

On the way they met Aunt Sarah and their mother. Their aunt exclaimed, "Freddie! Have you been swimming with your clothes on?"

Both Bert and Freddie had to laugh at this, and Harry teased, "Freddie just went in to play with the frogs!"

Mrs. Bobbsey guessed that the ducking was not intentional. "I think that the bathtub is the next stop for you, Freddie," she said. "Up you go! It's bedtime anyway. There's a big day ahead tomorrow."

Flossie was found in the barn saying good night to the kittens, and both children went upstairs to bed.

The next morning both the Bobbsey families were at the breakfast table early, fresh and ready for a day at the fair. Aunt Sarah, after her morning greeting, said ruefully, "I'm afraid that I can't go with you today. I have peaches that must be preserved at once or they'll spoil. You all go ahead without me."

Mrs. Bobbsey spoke up quickly. "Why can't the fathers go with the children today? I'd love to stay and help you."

Uncle Daniel looked at the eager faces of the

children and smiled as he replied, "I guess we can take that responsibility, eh, Dick? All aboard for the Bolton County Fair!"

The twins and Harry cheered, and after breakfast they all ran out to the station wagon. It was a beautiful sunny day with white clouds scudding across a deep blue sky. Soon the Bobbseys arrived at the fair grounds, which were humming with laughing, pushing crowds of people. Above the noise came the thin, wheezy notes of the calliope.

"Billy's already at work," remarked Bert as they made their way through the busy lanes toward the sound.

They found the merry-go-round whirling with a happy child on each animal while Billy played one lively tune after another. Mr. Bates was tending the boiler, and when Mr. Bobbsey asked for Ben Fagan he said regretfully, "I'm sorry, Ben isn't here. He had a bad toothache and has gone to a dentist over at Boonville. I don't expect him back until tonight."

The merry-go-round came slowly to a halt, and the younger twins were up on their chosen mounts as soon as the other riders got off them.

"Watch me on this golden tiger, Daddy!" shouted Flossie, wreathed in smiles.

"And me on my lion," cried Freddie, astride

a handsome, orange-colored beast. "I'm going to get the brass ring!" he boasted.

Nan chose a pale blue Arabian horse with golden reins, while Bert and Harry hopped onto dashing pinto ponies of scarlet and white.

Off they went, up and down, round and round to the joyous sound of the whistling organ. None of the Bobbseys was able to catch the brass ring. When the ride was over, they went to talk to Billy as he waited for the next group to take their seats on the merry-go-round. Mr. Bobbsey and Uncle Daniel had already spoken to Billy and were standing beside him as the others came up.

Mr. Bobbsey was saying, "That's good. I think Ben Fagan will give you better treatment—at least for a while. In the meantime I'm conducting a little investigation. By the way, I wanted to ask him about a camera of Bert's that's been missing ever since the picnic. Do you think Ben could have taken it?"

Nan thought that she saw a frightened look for a second in Billy's eyes as he heard this but he said only, "I'm sorry, Mr. Bobbsey. I haven't seen anything like that around here." Just then Mr. Bates called to Billy to start the music.

"We'll see you tomorrow," called Bert.

Uncle Daniel wanted to show them his sheep

on exhibition, so they headed toward the live-
stock tent. There were so many things to see
and so many people in the lanes between the
booths that the Bobbseys made slow progress.

A man was selling whistles that shrieked and
shot forth a paper tongue nearly a foot long.
These fascinated Flossie and Freddie so much
that Mr. Bobbsey bought them each one.

"As long as you keep them on your own level,"
he told them, "you may blow them. Don't go
around frightening people, though."

As they waited in line to get into the live-
stock exhibit, Freddie and Flossie amused themselves by blowing the whistles at each other.
When they got inside the tent, Flossie ran ahead
to walk with her father. Freddie became caught
up in the crowd pressing toward the exit.

Suddenly finding himself pushed outside
the exhibition tent, he thought, "Well, I'm not
going to try to get back in. I'll just wait around
here for them. They're bound to find me."

The little boy strolled along the lane between
the tents and open booths and stopped to peer
into the tent where fruits and vegetables were on
display. An enormous pumpkin on a low shelf
caught his eye. "I wonder if I can lift that?" he
asked himself.

Joining the group of sightseers who were filing into the tent, he made his way over to the pumpkin. He bent down quickly and put his arms around it, then tried to lift it. The pumpkin did not budge. He tried again and managed to move the huge orange globe, but to his horror it rolled off the ledge and across to the edge of the tent.

Several people turned to look at the little boy, and he reddened with embarrassment. Quickly he ran out of the tent and down the lane until he felt sure no one was coming after him.

When he stopped running he found that he was near a group of low white buildings surrounded by a fence. Beyond the buildings he spied a race track.

"Stables! Horses!" Freddie thought excitedly. "White Star must be in there. I think I'll go visit him!"

The little boy went carefully along the fence looking for a space wide enough to crawl through. In a few minutes he found a board missing next to a broken one. A small pile of new lumber was stacked nearby.

"It's a good thing they haven't fixed this hole," Freddie said to himself. "I'll just go right in here."

In another moment he had climbed through and stood looking about him. He was behind the stables.

All at once he heard low voices and saw that two men were standing on the other side of the lumber pile. They had their backs to Freddie, but one of them looked familiar. As the little boy watched, the man took a roll of bills from his pocket and slipped it into the hand of his companion. This second man was very short and wore a bright green jacket.

Just then the big man turned. "Why, it's Mr. Fagan!" Freddie thought in surprise. He was tempted to tell the man that Mr. Bobbsey wanted to ask him about the missing camera.

But as he hesitated Freddie caught sight of White Star himself! The horse was being led by a groom into one of the stalls. Freddie forgot everything else as he dashed through the narrow alleyway.

The little boy followed the two into the stall. The soft-soled shoes which he wore made no noise, and as he kept between the horse and the wall the stableman had no way of knowing Freddie was there.

The groom tied White Star securely, then gave him a pat on the flank. "There you are, old boy. Now have a good rest," he said and left the stall.

Freddie reached up to stroke the velvety black neck, and White Star looked down at him with soft, dark eyes. Then he put his head out to nuzzle Freddie's hand.

"Oh! You remember that sugar lump, don't you, White Star?"

Freddie was delighted that the horse had not forgotten him, but was sorry that he had no sugar. He stood for a moment wondering if he dared go back to the vegetable exhibit and get a carrot. Would the attendant recognize him as the boy who had rolled the pumpkin off the platform?

As he considered this, he heard a faint sound of rustling straw. Was someone entering the stall? By bending over, Freddie could see boots coming slowly across the floor toward the horse. Quietly, Freddie bent over still farther. Now he saw that it was the man in the green jacket. On his hands were dark gloves, and in one he carried a heavy wrench.

As the man crept nearer, Freddie suddenly realized that he planned to hurt White Star!

CHAPTER VIII

A SUSPICIOUS GAME

WHEN Freddie realized that White Star was in danger, his heart beat so hard he thought that the man on the other side of the horse would surely hear it.

"Maybe I can scare that bad man away!" he thought desperately.

The little boy put his hands into his pockets to steady himself, and his cold fingers touched the paper whistle. Quickly he put it to his mouth and blew with all his might, bending forward under the horse as he did so. The paper tongue darted out under White Star.

The shrill scream of the whistle and the snakelike whip of the paper startled White Star. Whinnying loudly, the horse reared up and pawed at the air. The crouching man, terrified, fell backward onto the straw-covered floor.

Freddie dropped the whistle with a start and flattened himself against the wall to avoid the flying hoofs. He could see the man in the green jacket plainly now, sprawled on the floor of the stall. He looked so comical that Freddie would have laughed had he not been frightened.

A number of stablemen came running to see what had disturbed White Star. One, ahead of the others, called out, "What's going on here?"

Then he spied the man with the wrench trying to crawl behind a bale of straw. He strode toward him shouting to the others, "Look who's here! Tony Lenaro with a wrench!"

Another groom cried out, "What are you doing here? Trying to lame the best horse in the race? You'd better explain, Tony!"

In a moment they had the short man on his feet and were dragging him out when another man rushed into the stall. He, too, was short and slight, and wore a scarlet jacket striped with white. He called angrily after the man who would have hurt White Star. "You can go to jail for this, Tony. What's the matter with you, anyway?"

Then the man in scarlet went to examine the trembling horse. "It's all right, my beauty. He's gone. Nothing will hurt you now," he said soothingly, and patted the arching neck. "You scared the rascal out of his wits anyway. How did you do it?" He chuckled as he bent to look at Star's leg.

Freddie decided it was time to come from his hiding place. He went softly around behind the horse and stopped beside the kneeling man. "I didn't mean to scare White Star," he said shyly. "I didn't think he'd be so frightened. I just wanted to stop that bad man before he hit him with that wrench."

The man had jumped up at Freddie's words and stood staring at the little boy as though he were a ghost. Freddie pointed to the whistle. "I did it with this."

The man laughed. "Well, good for you! I can't believe it. What are you doing here?" He took Freddie by the arm as he spoke and began to lead him out of the stall.

"I was at the fair. I came to see White Star," Freddie explained, as he was marched along by the stables and out to the attendant at the gate.

"This boy is lost, I guess," the little man told him. "I found the kid in White Star's stall. Where are your folks?" he asked Freddie.

Freddie waved his arm toward the fair grounds. "Over there. I'm sorry I scared White Star," he added, hanging his head.

"Maybe this is the boy those folks have been

looking for," the gateman said. "There goes his father now. Hey, mister, is this your son?"

Freddie saw his father and Nan hurrying toward him. Mr. Bobbsey looked very relieved when he saw Freddie.

Nan turned to call out to Bert and Flossie, who were farther back in the crowd. "Here he is. Tell Uncle Daniel we've found Freddie."

Mr. Bobbsey took Freddie's hand. "You must stay with us," he told him. "There are such crowds here today that it's easy to become separated from each other. Now tell us where you've been."

The little boy's story amazed everyone, and Mr. Bobbsey remarked, "This is serious business."

At that moment Bert broke in with, "Dad! It's almost time for the old-time balloon ascension. We'll have to hurry, or we'll miss it."

He and Harry started off on a run toward the balloon station. The others followed as fast as they could. They arrived just as the great rose-colored balloon rose into the air.

Freddie was very excited as his eyes followed its flight. "Where is it going?" he asked. "Is there anyone inside?"

Uncle Daniel answered, "There are two men in that little square basket under the big gas bag.

You're lucky to see this balloon, Freddie. They aren't shown very often."

"How do they steer it?" Freddie asked.

"They can't really guide it at all," Uncle Daniel answered. "The balloon is filled with a certain gas, and they gauge the time it will stay in the air by the amount of gas. The direction it takes depends on the wind."

"What an adventure to ride in one!" Bert exclaimed. "I'd like to go up in the balloon, wouldn't you, Harry?"

Harry shook his head. "I'll take a jet plane that I can steer," he replied, laughing.

As the rose-colored mushroom disappeared over a hill, Bert said, "Dad, isn't it time for lunch?"

"Yes. Let's go on over to the refreshment tent. Afterward we can visit some of the other concessions and watch the horse race."

"What's concessions, Nan?" asked Flossie, as they went toward the dining tent.

"They're the booths that you see on each side of the streets here," Nan explained. "People from all over come to county fairs to sell produce."

Mr. Bobbsey, who was just behind them, added, "They come here to set up amusement stands, too, like shooting galleries."

"That's one I want to try," Uncle Daniel said. "I used to be a pretty good shot."

"Me, too," cried Bert.

Just then they met a clown selling funny paper hats, and Uncle Daniel bought five. Nan's and Flossie's were bonnets with tall, wired red roses, while the boys got caps with clown faces. The children put their hats on immediately.

"This is like Hallowe'en!" Flossie said, giggling.

There was one line of people waiting at the entrance to the refreshment tent and another of outgoing patrons. The lines were separated by a thin rope. Nan, standing next to this barrier, was suddenly pushed by a large woman in the outgoing line. The girl's paper bonnet was knocked from her head.

"Beg pardon, miss," the woman said, as Nan bent to catch the bonnet before it was trampled underfoot. "There's a man trying to get ahead of everybody, and he pushed me."

Nan smiled and was about to speak when she saw that the man in a hurry was Ben Fagan. She pulled at her father's sleeve, and Mr. Bobbsey turned. It was obvious that Ben Fagan did not want to be seen by the Bobbseys, but before he could get away the twins' father called to him.

"Oh, Mr. Fagan, will you stop for a moment? I'd like a word with you."

The man pretended not to hear, but a woman planted herself in his way, saying, "That gentleman is calling you. Don't you hear him?"

Reluctantly Ben Fagan came to the rope. Mr. Bobbsey lifted it so that the man could stoop underneath. They moved with the crowd and came into the dining tent.

"What do you want?" Ben Fagan asked curtly.

Mr. Bobbsey answered in a low tone, "I've been wanting to ask you about a camera of my son's which disappeared the day of the picnic at Pine Grove."

The face of the merry-go-round man turned a deep red, but he answered boldly, "I don't know anything about it. You'd better ask Billy if you think it was stolen."

Bert, who was standing beside him, spoke up quickly, "We did ask Billy. He doesn't know anything about it."

Ben Fagan smirked and said, "I wouldn't be too sure about that. I saw him with a new camera yesterday."

Nan and Bert were angry at this remark. They were sure that Billy was not a thief.

Mr. Bobbsey said sharply, "How do you know that the camera was new? I didn't say that it was."

For a moment Ben Fagan looked confused. Then Freddie saved him from answering that question by asking another. "Who was that you were giving money to in back of the stable, Mr. Fagan?"

The calliope man looked as though he had just received an electric shock. Then, putting his hand to his cheek, he muttered something about a toothache, darted under the rope, and sped out of the tent.

"What happened to him?" Nan asked. "He acted as though a hornet had stung him."

Uncle Daniel laughed. "Freddie's question

must have carried a sting. We'll have to hear more about this."

A waiter showed the Bobbseys to a table. As they ate, Freddie told of having seen Fagan and the green-jacketed man together.

"Sounds like some kind of suspicious deal," Bert commented.

The men agreed. "Fagan did seem uneasy," the twins' father said. "He'll bear watching."

The Bobbseys found that they were very hungry and enjoyed the home-cooked farm food. After they left the refreshment tent the sightseers wandered along the main thoroughfare until they came to the shooting gallery.

"Now we'll see who can get the most prizes, Harry," cried Bert. "You and I can match each other. I'm afraid we aren't in our dads' class."

"I s'pose I'm not big enough to shoot those guns." Freddie sighed.

"We'll find something else for you to do," Nan told him. "Look! Here's a ball-throwing game right next door. Let's try that."

In charge of the booth was a bored-looking man who sold them each five balls for a dime. He pointed to a canvas curtain hung across the back of the booth. On it was painted a huge clown face with small eyes and a tiny, half-opened mouth.

"You have to get all the balls in the mouth to win a prize," he told them.

"You take the first turn, Flossie," Nan said.

All of Flossie's balls fell short of the mark. Then Freddie threw two balls which struck the target but fell back without going inside the mouth. His next three hit the flat cheeks and big nose of the painted face.

"Too bad, Freddie," Nan said as she picked up a ball, "I thought your first two hit the mouth squarely. I don't see why they didn't go in."

She aimed carefully and threw her first ball straight at the target. It struck the half-opened mouth of the back drop and bounced back to fall on the floor. The second one did the same.

Nan turned to the man in charge, who was looking on with a sly grin on his face. "There's something there that won't let the ball go in," she insisted. "That's not fair!"

He laughed loudly and walked over to the curtain. "Nonsense," he said, thrusting his hand into the painted mouth. "See? I can put my whole hand inside. You just don't know how to hit it right."

He returned to his place at the side and Nan picked up her third ball. As she looked at the target she was startled to see that the eyes of the painted face were looking directly at her and seemed as real as her own!

CHAPTER IX

BALLOON ADRIFT!

"OH!" Nan exclaimed and dropped her ball.

After she picked it up and again faced the target, the eyes no longer looked real but were as painted as the face. Nan decided not to mention her scare to the little twins. "Maybe I'm just imagining things," she told herself.

She threw the ball, and to her surprise, it disappeared into the mouth. The fourth and fifth did the same.

"There! You see?" the concession man cried. "Now you're beginning to get the hang of it. Buy some more balls and try again. Maybe you'll win a prize."

"No, thank you," Nan replied, turning away. She wanted to leave the booth as fast as possible. The memory of the eyes behind the curtain made her feel uncomfortable.

Bert had won a silly-looking lady doll at the shooting gallery. He presented it to Flossie, and Harry gave Freddie a small airplane which he had been awarded. The fathers were laden with bowls and baskets, for the two were excellent marksmen.

"I think it's about time for us to go home," Uncle Daniel suggested. "We can't carry all this stuff around with us."

"What about the horse race?" Freddie asked. "I want to see White Star run."

"We'll go past the field," Uncle Daniel said. "I think the horses are just practicing for to-night's races."

When they arrived, Freddie at once spotted White Star. "Look at him go! He can beat any horse!" the little boy cried.

The sleek black animal was racing around the track at a good clip. As he passed the Bobbseys, they cheered.

A man who stood near them with a stop watch in his hand said, "You know how to pick 'em, sonny. White Star ought to win the big race that's coming up day after tomorrow. He sure made fast time today."

As the Bobbseys moved off, Bert patted Freddie on the shoulder. "But White Star wouldn't have run at all if it hadn't been for you!"

Freddie beamed proudly. "That was my scare-em toy." He grinned.

When the Bobbseys reached Meadowbrook, they scrambled out of the station wagon. Mrs. Bobbsey and Aunt Sarah had set some lemonade and cookies on a little table under the big elms. The children threw themselves on the ground while the grownups settled in lawn chairs. It was cool and delightful after the heat and glare of the fair grounds.

The various adventures at the county fair were related. The women were amazed to hear them, and Mrs. Bobbsey remarked that she did not like the various things Ben Fagan had done.

"I don't either," the twins' father agreed.

Uncle Daniel spoke up, "Dick, let's go over to see John Gardner. He lives just down the road and is one of the best lawyers in the county. I'm sure he can give us some good advice about this situation of Billy's."

Mr. Bobbsey agreed, and the two men left the house directly after supper. The children were asleep by the time the men returned. The next morning Bert hoped to hear something about the lawyer, but neither his father nor his uncle spoke of it.

The day was cool with strong winds blowing gray clouds across the sky. Nevertheless the Bobbseys left early for the fair. They used two cars since this time they all went. Because of the weather they carried sweaters, coats, and slickers.

"I don't hear the calliope," Bert remarked as they reached the county fair and walked toward the entrance.

"The bad weather may have kept many people away today," Mr. Bobbsey said.

Uncle Daniel paused when they reached the gate. "I'd like to see how my sheep are. They're very sensitive creatures, you know."

"I'll go with you, Dad," Harry decided.

Aunt Sarah hesitated for a moment, then laughed and said, "I think I'll join the twins. I must meet this Billy Fagan and hear him play the calliope."

"Let's get together at the balloon station at eleven," Bert suggested to his cousin and uncle. "That's when they send up the balloon."

"Okay. Fine," Harry agreed.

They parted and the twins went with their parents and Aunt Sarah. The merry-go-round was standing idle. Billy Fagan was nearby, looking very pale and worried. His face lighted up when he saw his friends.

Before Bert had a chance to introduce him to Aunt Sarah, Billy said in a low voice, "I have some important news, Bert. Last night—"

"Billy! Get busy on that calliope!" Ben

Fagan's harsh voice broke in, as he came rapidly out of a tent nearby. He was striding angrily toward the two boys when he saw Mr. Bobbsey. Fagan turned and started back to the tent.

But Mr. Bobbsey called to him, "Oh, Mr. Fagan! Wait a minute." He walked toward the man, but Fagan kept on going.

"This won't take long," Mr. Bobbsey told him as he caught up to Fagan. "You have some explaining to do about Billy. I've engaged a lawyer to listen to your story tomorrow morning."

The other man whirled around. "What do you mean?" he demanded in a loud voice.

"I've done some investigating," Mr. Bobbsey said quietly.

Ben Fagan's face flushed, and his little eyes gleamed with anger. After a moment, however, he spoke in a soft, wheedling tone. "Look, Mr. Bobbsey, I can't be bothered now. I got to get that merry-go-round going. You're making yourself a lot of trouble over nothing."

"I think not," Mr. Bobbsey said as Fagan left. "I'll be back with the lawyer tomorrow."

There was a sly smile on Fagan's face as he answered, "Sure, sure."

Then he went to tinker with the motor of the merry-go-round and stoke the steam boiler.

Before long the younger twins mounted their prancing animals, and the machinery started. A few other children had come to ride on the merry-go-round. Away they went!

Bert had introduced Billy to Aunt Sarah while his father talked to Ben Fagan. Now they stood listening to the calliope.

"I'm chilly even with a warm coat on," Aunt Sarah whispered to Mrs. Bobbsey, "and that poor boy Billy hasn't anything over his thin shirt."

"I know!" Bert exclaimed. "I'll lend him my extra sweater, Mother. I have my slicker to use."

His mother smiled and nodded, so Bert ran to put his sweater over the boy's shoulders. Billy protested, but Bert ran off to join Nan in a turn on the merry-go-round. The younger twins went round once again with them.

Bert told Nan, "I didn't have a chance to talk to Billy, but I did tell him we'd try to come back before we leave. He says he has something important to tell me," Bert finished.

The wind was rising rapidly as the Bobbseys made their way along the aisles of the fair. Papers blown from the booths were whisked across their path while the owners tried frantically to fasten down their decorations and light articles.

"Won't you buy some candy?" cried one lady

as they passed. "I'll have to put it away in a minute, because I can't keep it covered against the wind."

The candy looked so good that Nan bought a bagful and tucked it into her coat pocket to eat after lunch.

"I doubt if there will be a balloon ascension," Mr. Bobbsey was saying as Nan came up. "With this terrifically strong wind it would be sheer folly."

When the Bobbsey group arrived at the balloon station, they found it a scene of noisy confusion. Men were shouting as they struggled to hold the inflated gas bag in place.

"Bring more sandbags, on the double!"

"Hey, lend me a hand with this cable here!"

A fine rain began to whip across the fair grounds, and the Bobbseys hastened to slip on their raincoats. As Mrs. Bobbsey fastened the ties of Flossie's rain hat under her chin, the little girl asked:

"Won't there be a 'cension today?"

One of the men who was struggling to hold the balloon to its moorings overheard her question. He laughed and said, "Not if we can help it, but the balloon sure is fighting to go."

All of the men at the ropes were working on the far side of the big bag. Freddie and Flossie strolled away from the others for a closer look at the basket, which rested near them. No one else noticed when the little boy clambered up the side and peered down into its depths.

"It's nice in there," Freddie reported to his twin. "I saw blankets and pillows and a box of crackers and what looked like a water bottle. Let's get in and pretend we're the balloon men."

Flossie giggled and followed her adventurous brother to the sturdy, square wicker basket. They clambered up its side and hopped down onto the floor of the basket. Here, sheltered from the wind and rain, it was warm and cozy.

The other members of the Bobbsey family watched Uncle Daniel and Harry, who were making slow progress across the field. Finally they reached the others.

"Wait until you hear what Dad has to tell you!" shouted Harry when they were near enough to make themselves heard. "It's great news!"

As he spoke, a sudden gust of wind swept his rain hat from his head, and it went whirling and bumping across the wet grass. Bert sprang to help his cousin chase it, but at that moment a shout rang out:

"Look out! There she goes!"

Everyone turned to stare at the balloon. The

Freddie and Flossie climbed up the side of the basket

powerful blast of wind which had carried away Harry's hat had torn the straining gas bag from its moorings. With a loud snap of breaking rope it shot up into the air.

As the balloon hung for a moment above them, the startled watchers saw two small heads in yellow oilskin hats appear over the brim of the basket.

"Freddie and Flossie!" screamed Nan.

CHAPTER X

AN EXCITING RIDE

THE sudden lurch and upward swing of the balloon as it tore itself loose had severely frightened the small twins.

Flossie and Freddie had been snuggled under the waterproof blanket at the bottom of the basket, pretending they were traveling high in the air across the jungles of Africa. But now they were terrified to find themselves really swinging through the air.

Both children rushed to climb up and look over the edge of the basket. Far below them they saw the upturned faces of their family and the men who had been trying to hold the balloon to the ground.

Flossie burst out crying and clutched her twin's arm. "Oh, I want to get down!" she screamed.

Freddie was just as frightened as she was, but he said in a very brave voice, "They'll get us to the ground all right, Flossie. Don't worry."

"They can't," she answered, wiping her eyes and trying to be as brave as her twin brother. "We'll just have to wait 'til the balloon is unscensioned."

"I guess you're right," Freddie agreed. "They'll follow us, though, and be there when it does come down."

The twins were being blown wildly through the air, and by now the fair grounds were almost out of sight.

"Let's get down under the blanket again. We might be blown out if we stand up here," Freddie suggested. "The wind is taking the breath right out of my mouth!"

As they settled themselves again away from the rain and the wind, Flossie remarked with a sob, "It's awfully bumpy, Freddie! Do you think we'll get tossed out of the basket?"

He took her hand in his to comfort her. "You hang onto me, Flossie, and you'll be all right. I'm sure the basket is fixed so it won't turn over. The balloon men must have thought of that."

"Oh yes, of course. I forgot they ride in here every day!" exclaimed his twin. She was happier now.

"If it wasn't so bumpy and windy I'd look over the edge and try to see our station wagon. I'm sure it must be racing us along the road," Freddie told her confidently.

Flossie caught at his sleeve. "No!" she cried. "Don't stand up now. You might be blown out!"

Freddie giggled. "Wouldn't the folks be surprised if I were and landed right on top of the station wagon? Wow!"

They both laughed at that, and Flossie felt relieved as she thought of the family car traveling along just below the balloon. She knew that her father would be waiting whenever and wherever they came to the ground.

The balloon was plunging about and jerking the lines which held the basket to the huge gas bag.

"Those wires are very strong, Flossie," her brother assured her as they gazed upward anxiously.

Flossie nodded. The swaying of the basket made her very drowsy, now that she was not so frightened, and presently she was fast asleep with her head on Freddie's shoulder. He sat very still and soon he, too, was dozing lightly.

When he awoke the rain had stopped, and there was less wind. The balloon was drifting lazily across the sky, and Freddie thought that it was lower, but he had no way of telling. He wanted to climb up and look out over the basket's edge, but he sat quietly for a few moments for fear of waking Flossie. Then, because he was a little afraid, he decided that he just had to see what lay below them. As he moved to get up, Flossie awoke.

"I'm going to look over and see where we are," he told her. "The rain's stopped."

She nodded and watched as he climbed up the side of the basket. "I'm coming to look, too," she said, and scrambled to her feet.

Freddie gazed downward through heavy folds of mist. He could hear something below that sounded like water swishing, and his eyes strained to see through the fog. Just as Flossie arrived beside him, the clouds of mist parted for a moment, and he caught sight of a strip of gray water directly beneath them.

Flossie had seen it, too. "Oooooh! There's water down there!" she cried in a frightened voice.

"I g-guess so," Freddie answered shakily. Then he added, "We can both swim, though."

"Not too far," she told him, trembling. "Oh, Freddie, I'm scared!"

"Maybe the basket will float," he said hopefully.

They slid down and sat again at the bottom of the basket. Freddie carefully watched the rose-colored balloon. It was certainly much smaller than it had been when they left the fair grounds, and the glimpse of water had shown the twins that they were not as high in the air as before.

"How can Daddy find us if we go down on the water?" Flossie asked fearfully.

"I don't know," her twin answered truthfully. Then he added cheerfully, "But Daddy will find a way. He always does. We'll just swim around and float when we're tired until a boat comes. I'm going to look again and see how close we are to the water now."

Freddie got to his feet but sat down again very hard as the basket gave a lurch and something scraped its underside. After a few more bounces it bumped along roughly, and the twins could hear the breaking of branches. Then the basket suddenly turned over.

The twins were tossed out and landed on a bed of wet leaves!

"Land!" screamed Freddie excitedly.

"It's almost as wet as water," Flossie said as she sat up and brushed the soaked leaves from her hair. "But I'm so glad we're down!"

Freddie stood listening and looking about

him through the fog. "I hear waves right near by," he said. "The sound comes from over there." The little boy pointed. "Maybe this is an island."

Flossie tried to peer through the mist also. "We were out over that water!"

The twins suddenly noticed that the cables attached to the basket lay limp on the ground. Flossie looked about, puzzled.

"The balloon must have broken away before we landed," she said. "But where is it?"

The children scanned the area as well as they could in the fog, which was still dense.

"There it is!" cried Freddie.

He pointed to a short but sturdy maple nearby. Entwined in its branches was the now deflated balloon. The twins stared upward at its rose-colored folds.

"I wouldn't want to ride in that again," Freddie said. "But it was sort of fun after all."

Flossie shook her wet curls. "I'll never ride in a balloon again, ever!" she announced firmly. "I'm hungry! Did we eat all of the crackers in that box?"

Freddie nodded, then pointed to a dark mass through the swirling mist. "Those are thick woods," he told her. "It will be dry in there, and maybe we can find some nuts or berries to eat."

They gathered up their rain hats and ran toward the grove. As they came nearer they could see that it was a large patch of evergreen woods carpeted with pine needles.

Flossie sat down on the ground. "It's dry!" she exclaimed. "And it smells good!"

Freddie was looking around for nuts but found none. "I guess there aren't any here with all these fir trees." he said sadly.

He walked a little farther. Then Flossie heard him squeal happily. "These are blueberry bushes, and there are lots of berries on them!"

She scrambled to her feet and ran to a clearing where her twin stood picking the ripe fruit.

"Yum, yum!" Flossie murmured when Freddie gave her some of the berries. "They taste good even without cream and sugar."

Freddie crammed a small handful into his cheeks so that he looked like a chipmunk. As soon as he could speak, he said, "I think there may be more berries on those bushes over beyond that big tree. I'll go pick those, and you can have the rest of these."

He moved away and Flossie stayed to strip the berries from their hiding places under the glossy leaves. The little girl took off her sou'wester, thinking she would use it to hold the fruit. At the same moment she heard a rustling sound on the other side of the thicket.

"That must be Freddie," she thought in surprise. "He's back already." Aloud she asked, "Didn't you find any berries over there?"

Just then, to her great astonishment, Freddie's voice came to her from a distance. "Hey, Flossie! I see a cabin through the woods! There must be a beach around here, too. I can't see it but I hear the waves," he cried.

Flossie's answer died in her throat. At that moment the head of a large brown bear appeared over the top of the thicket directly in front of her.

For a moment the two remained motionless, staring at each other. Then Flossie took to her heels, dropping rain hat and berries in her fright. She ran stumbling in the direction of Freddie's voice. The little girl could hear the bear crashing through the underbrush behind her.

"Flossie, come on!" Freddie called again. "Let's go see—" Then he heard his sister scream and raced toward her. When he saw the bear lumbering behind Flossie, Freddie grabbed his twin's hand.

"Hurry!" he gasped, pulling her along. "The —the cabin's just ahead."

They dashed over the rough ground, the bear in close pursuit. Reaching the cabin, the children hurled themselves against the heavy door. It swung open on squeaking hinges and they almost fell inside.

Then the twins pushed the door shut and bolted it. The next second they heard the bear growl and place his heavy paws on the other side of the door.

CHAPTER XI

THE SEARCH PARTY

BACK at the fair grounds, Mr. and Mrs. Bobbsey and the older twins could scarcely believe their eyes at the sight of Freddie and Flossie being blown away in the balloon. They stared in horror at the faces of the two children looking down at them from the basket.

Then Mrs. Bobbsey screamed. "Oh! Get them down! Get them down!" she cried to the men at the ropes.

One of the attendants rushed off to a telephone. The other came hurrying up to the Bobbseys. "Are those your children?" he asked. "How did they get in the basket?"

Mr. Bobbsey answered quickly, "Yes, they're ours. I suppose they simply climbed in. But the important question now is how are we to rescue them? Where's the nearest helicopter?"

The man shrugged. "The one that's usually here at the airport is on emergency duty in the next county. Wouldn't do any good anyway," he added. "It would be better to let the balloon take its course than to try getting the children out of the basket in mid-air. I'm Alfred Carter, and that man coming from the building is my brother Horace. We own the balloon so we're as worried as you are."

"What can we do, Mr. Carter?" Mrs. Bobbsey asked frantically.

"The balloon had about enough gas to carry it aloft for two hours," the man replied. "The wind is from the west, so it will be blown due east."

Aunt Sarah, who had been listening intently, exclaimed, "That would take it out over Long Lake! It's just east of here."

"That's what we figured, ma'am," Alfred Carter agreed. "My brother is trying to find a boat."

At this moment Horace Carter came up to the group. "I've located a boat, called *Nellie*, on Long Lake," he said. "The skipper will be ready to start the search as soon as we get there. There's room for you, Mr. Bobbsey, if you wish to come."

"Indeed I do!" the twins' father exclaimed. "How many can you take?"

"It's a good-sized fishing boat," Horace Carter replied. "I should think we could take four besides ourselves, but you'll have to hurry!"

Daniel Bobbsey put his hand on his brother's shoulder. "You four go, Dick. Sarah and I will be waiting for you at Meadowbrook with a big supper when you all come back."

As Alfred Carter started off he shouted back over the wind to Mr. Bobbsey, "Turn left at the fair grounds gate, and take the highway. Follow it to the first light. Turn left again to Bankston. We'll meet you there at the wharf."

The Bobbseys hurried out to the parking lot in the wind and rain. Uncle Daniel, Aunt Sarah, and Harry called out good-bys and hopes of good luck as the two cars parted company at the highway.

"We're making good time," Bert observed as he looked at his watch. "It was quarter of twelve when you were talking to Mr. Carter, Dad, and it's just twelve now."

The car sped along the road as the Bobbseys searched the sky for some sign of the runaway balloon.

"The wind seems to be dying down," remarked Mrs. Bobbsey, "but the air is very heavy and misty."

They had turned at the light and were soon

on the streets of a small fishing town.

Mr. Bobbsey looked along the waterfront. "Mr. Carter spoke as though there was only one wharf, but I see four or five small piers."

"I see the *Nellie*, Dad," Bert cried. "Just beyond that old gray shack."

"There's a car right behind us," Nan remarked. "I think the Carters are in it."

The two cars drove onto the wharf where they were met by a weather-toughened group of men in oilskins. The oldest man, who seemed to have charge of the group, stepped forward. "I'm Captain North," he said.

Horace Carter introduced himself, his brother, and the Bobbseys to the captain, who said, "Too bad about that balloon floatin' off. Can't see any farther over water than a cat's nose now, but we'll do our best to spot it."

The sturdy seaman then led the way aboard his trim fishing launch. The fog grew even more dense as the boat moved out on the water. It seemed as though a heavy curtain spread before the *Nellie*.

"Can't make much time today," the captain grumbled.

"Was the balloon sighted from Bankston?" Alfred Carter asked.

"I didn't see it," Captain North told him. "But

one of the crew of a fishin' boat which just came in said he'd seen a big red object up in the sky."

"How long ago was that?" Mr. Bobbsey asked, straining his eyes to pierce the blanket of fog.

"I'd say about half, three quarters of an hour ago. Are all you folks balloon people?"

"No," Horace Carter replied. "Captain North, two of the Bobbsey children are adrift in that balloon!"

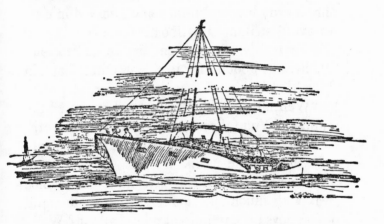

The captain was so startled that he nearly lost control of the wheel. "Jumping mackerel!" he shouted. "Why didn't you say so? Step 'er up, Hank!" The man at the engine sang out, "Aye, Aye!" and the *Nellie* picked up speed.

"We'll find those kids!" the captain declared firmly.

Nan sat forward, staring into the fog and listening for any sound from over the water. A faint, muffled splash just ahead sent her heart racing. Suddenly she saw, directly in front of the launch, the outline of another boat.

"Ahoy there! Don't run us down!" shouted a voice from the fog.

Captain North whirled the wheel rapidly as he gave directions to stop and reverse the engine. The sturdy launch lurched and swerved in time to avoid striking a sailboat.

One of the three men aboard called out, "Where you bound for in this weather, Captain North? It's sure pea soup out here."

"Well, at least I got a motor," answered the captain. "You fellows get caught in the storm?"

"Yes. But we'll make it okay. There's plenty of wind to take us in."

The captain shouted once more. His voice was very much like a foghorn, Nan thought. "You boys see anything of a big balloon? We're looking for one that's got a couple of children aboard."

"Sufferin' codfish!" exclaimed a sailor as he turned the sloop back into the wind. "Yes, we saw something when the mist was coming in. Could have been a balloon. It was heading toward Hemlock."

"Thanks," Mr. Bobbsey called.

The captain spun the steering wheel once more, and the launch veered into a new course. "Now we have something to go on," he cried heartily. "We'll head for Hemlock Island."

"Oh, I hope the balloon landed there safely!" said Nan.

"I was wondering, Mr. Carter," said Mrs. Bobbsey. "Would the basket float for a while if the balloon happened to come down on water?"

Alfred Carter looked doubtful, but his brother answered cheerfully, "It might, ma'am, for a short time. We've never tried it out."

"When a balloon comes down on solid ground," Bert questioned, "how does it make a landing? Does it drop gently?"

Alfred Carter answered thoughtfully. "That depends. Generally a balloon floats gently to the earth, but if it caught on something, like a pole, the gas bag might be punctured. Then it would drop quickly because the weights have nothing to balance them."

An expression of alarm crossed Mrs. Bobbsey's face at these words. Captain North said encouragingly to her, "There aren't any poles on Hemlock Island, ma'am, for balloons to hitch onto."

"I'm sure the twins' adventure will have a

happy ending, dear," said Mr. Bobbsey to his wife, a ring of conviction in his voice.

"I hope you are right, Dick." Mrs. Bobbsey smiled wanly.

Nan, meanwhile, stuck to her post in the bow of the boat, looking and listening intently. Except for the motor, there was deep silence all around them. It was almost as though, she imagined, they were shut away from the rest of the world by the fog.

Bert stood near the rail, his eyes and ears also alert. He was impatient to reach the island and begin the search for Flossie and Freddie.

"Reduce speed, Hank," Captain North directed presently. "We can't be far from Hemlock, and I haven't any wheels under the *Nellie* so I want to stop while I'm still on water!"

"Ha, ha," Hank laughed. "That's a good one! The *Nellie's* got no wheels!"

"That's no joke," said the captain in a sober tone. "We're near the point of Hemlock Island, and there are rocks ahead."

At that moment, with a sudden grind and jolt, the launch came to an abrupt stop.

CHAPTER XII

LOST IN THE FOG

ABOUT this time Flossie and Freddie stood with their backs braced against the door of the island cabin. They could hear the bear sniffing and clawing at the crack between the sill and the bottom of the door. The twins feared that at any moment the animal would throw his weight against the worn boards.

"Anyway, he can't slip the bolt," Freddie whispered encouragingly. "And maybe he won't try to break the door down."

The twins waited, hardly daring to breathe. They glanced around the cabin which consisted of only one room with a single window. It was empty except for a roughly built table in the middle and a cot at one end. There were fish nets strung upon the wall, and several buckets stood on the floor and table. In one corner some fishing poles were stacked, and two pairs of oars were laid close to the wall.

Above the window was a shelf holding some large tin cans. One was marked PITCH, another LINE, and a third bore the word CORKS. The other two were turned so the twins could not see the labels.

"That one looks like a honey tin," whispered Flossie, pointing.

Freddie examined it from his place at the cabin door. "I think it *was* a honey tin, but I'll bet it has fish hooks or something like that in it now."

His twin sighed. "I s'pose so. I don't believe there's anything in this place to eat—"

"Sh!" Freddie poked her. "I think he's going away."

The sniffing and clawing had stopped, and the twins heard the loud snapping of twigs and underbrush as the bear went lumbering off through the woods.

"I hope he's gone away for good," Flossie said, going to the window. "Oh my! I can't see out at all. This is an awful dirty window!"

She rubbed at the pane vigorously and made a clear spot for one eye. "I can't see anything but a little of the beach and one tree right in front of the cabin," she said, squinting.

Freddie rubbed another spot on the pane. "I see a boat!" he exclaimed.

Flossie shrieked, "Where? Where?"

"Out there on the beach," Freddie told her calmly. "These oars must belong to it."

"Oh! A rowboat!" Flossie's eyes filled with tears. She had expected to see a boat with their father coming to their rescue. "Freddie, when do you think Daddy will come?"

"Well," he answered, turning away from the window, "he'll come as soon as he can find a way."

The little boy walked over to inspect a crude map that was drawn in heavy black lines on one wall.

"Look, Flossie. This is a map of an island, and I think it's this one. It says down here, 'Hemlock Island.' Those marks are meant to be fir trees like the ones in these woods and that little square is the cabin. See? And there's the beach."

"What are those peaked things?" asked Flossie, pointing to one end of the island on the map.

"I think those are rocks. Remember I said I heard waves somewhere when we were spilled out of the basket? I guess we were pretty close to those rocks then."

"Oooo!" Flossie shuddered.

Freddie was studying the map. "I believe this

is the place," he showed her a mark on the map, "where the balloon got caught on the maple tree."

The two children stared at the map for a few seconds. Then Freddie drew a long breath and remarked slowly, "Golly! We could have been tipped out into the water, or onto the rocks! I guess we're pretty lucky!"

Flossie nodded. "But I wish that old bear wasn't near here," she said. "And I wish Daddy would come. I'm afraid he won't be able to find us on this island."

Freddie had been thinking the same thing. But now he had a sudden idea. "I'll tell you what we'll do," he said. "We'll take those oars out and put them in the boat. Then I'll row us over to the mainland. There'll be houses there, and we can telephone to Uncle Daniel's farm and tell them where we are."

Flossie's face brightened. Then it clouded again as she said, "Oh, Freddie, you couldn't row that far."

"Yes, I can. Don't you remember that day at Pine Grove when I rowed all the way to the dock from in the middle of the lake?"

"Y-yes," she replied slowly. "But how will you know which way to go?"

"I'll find the way," he answered confidently.

"Come along." He got the oars and put them across his shoulders.

"Be sure the bear isn't outside," Flossie cautioned her twin.

They opened the door slowly, but the rusty hinges squeaked loudly. The children waited fearfully for any sound of breaking branches that might warn of the bear's return. Suddenly a hoarse wail rasped through the fog.

"What's that?" Flossie squealed, ready to run back into the cabin.

Freddie grinned. "It's just a foghorn, silly. I can follow the sound. We're bound to find someone there."

They hurried down a little slope to the beach where the flat-bottomed rowboat was drawn part way up on the sand. The twins removed their shoes and socks and put them in the boat. Freddie went back for the oars. They were heavy and awkward but he managed to put them into the oarlocks at last. Then the children began to push the boat with all their might. It was a struggle but the boat moved inch by inch over the sand.

The fear that the bear might come back gave the small twins extra energy. They knew the animal might follow their scent and the fog could keep them from seeing him until he was close by.

"Hurry! Hurry! Push harder!" Freddie urged.

At last the two children reached the water's edge. With a final push they floated the rowboat in deeper water and scrambled up over the sides.

Freddie, in the rower's seat, braced his feet on the next seat and began to pull on the long oars. It was very hard for him to handle them at first, but before long they were dipping in and out with regular strokes.

"I can't see the island any more," Flossie said at length. "It's too foggy."

The foghorn seemed farther away than before as it sounded its mournful warning. Freddie pulled harder upon his right oar. "The horn isn't straight ahead of us now," he remarked. "The sound came from over to the left this way."

Flossie tried to peer through the fog, but it was too dense. "S'pose there was a boat out here. We could bump right into it," she observed.

"We'd better yell once in a while, just to let people know where we are," Freddie advised.

"All right," Flossie opened her mouth wide and gave something between a scream and a shout.

"That'll scare them green," her twin said, giggling. "They'll think there's a sea monster around."

"My voice didn't seem loud at all," Flossie complained.

"I guess the fog swallows the sound," said her twin. Then Freddie added wearily, "I keep rowing straight for that foghorn, but it keeps moving around."

"Maybe it isn't a foghorn," Flossie replied. "It sounds more like an old cow to me."

Freddie laughed. He kept on rowing, but his arms were beginning to feel numb. Finally he pulled in the oars and sat looking unhappily at Flossie.

"We aren't getting anywhere," he said. "And I don't know where we are."

Flossie moved carefully over to sit beside him. "I'll take one of the oars," she offered. "Let's row back to the island and wait in the cabin 'til Daddy comes."

They turned the boat around and began to row. Flossie kept showering both children with water as she tried to manage the long, heavy oar. She either dipped too deeply and nearly lost it or hit the surface of the water. The little girl tried hard to match her stroke to Freddie's but it was very uneven rowing.

They stopped to listen as the fog warning came again. This time the sound seemed to be just ahead of the twins!

"We're not going toward the island!" Freddie cried. "It must be behind us instead of in front."

"Let's rest a minute," Flossie urged. She was puffing from the effort of rowing so hard. "Maybe the fog will go away pretty soon and then we can see where we are. Or perhaps the waves will carry us back to shore."

Freddie was willing to rest, but he did not think that the fog was going to lift soon. He knew, too, that such little waves would not take them ashore. The foghorn's wail came more faintly now.

Freddie gradually realized that the sound was not behind them but over to the right. "I'm afraid we're lost," he told Flossie. "I think we'd better yell some more while we're resting."

He cupped his hands around his mouth and shouted as hard as he could. Flossie did the same, but it seemed to them that the white fog blocked their voices.

"It's no use," the little girl said. She was on the verge of tears. "We can't make anybody hear us."

"Listen!" cried Freddie.

They both sat still as little statues. The fog-horn wailed hoarsely again behind them.

"I thought I heard someone calling," Freddie said. "Let's yell."

Once more they shouted at the top of their lungs into the thick air. The children waited anxiously, straining to hear the slightest sound. There was no answer.

"Come on, let's row." Freddie dipped his oar.

Flossie dipped hers, too, but the stroke was too shallow and sent a rainlike spray over them. She tried again and dipped so deep that her oar struck sand.

"Freddie!" she cried, "the water isn't deep here at all. We must be near shore!"

At that moment a muffled but familiar voice came through the fog. "Freddie! Flossie! Where are you?"

"Freddie!" exclaimed Flossie. "That sounds like Billy Fagan."

"It sure does," her twin agreed. "But what would he be doing here?"

"Maybe he came with Daddy to save us," Flossie said.

"We're out here," shouted Freddie. "On the water. Where are you?"

Only silence greeted the twins. Then came the barely audible response, "On the island."

"Oh dear," moaned Flossie. "We're not near shore any more."

"I must have rowed in circles," admitted Freddie. "But it's all right now," he said cheerfully. "I'll find the island."

"Freddie! Flossie! Can you hear me?"

To the children's joy, Billy's words were clearer.

"We're coming," Freddie shouted. He took both oars in a firm grip and began to pull with all his strength in the direction of Billy's voice.

CHAPTER XIII

THE BROWN BEAR

OUT ON the lake the sudden stop of the launch *Nellie* had thrown all her passengers off balance. Nan had fallen from the overturned bait barrel where she had been sitting. Bert had slipped on the coiled cable that lay on the deck. Quickly everyone regained his footing.

"We've hit the rocks!" Captain North shouted. "Everybody stay where you are!"

Ahead of them the Bobbseys could see the rocks, brown and wet, and through the fog, the dim outline of the shore. It looked bleak and forbidding rising out of the mist.

"What happens now?" Mr. Bobbsey asked in a worried tone.

"I'll have to see what damage has been done to the launch before I can put you ashore," the captain replied. He and another seaman slipped over the side of the *Nellie,* while Hank took the wheel.

"What a dreary spot!" Mrs. Bobbsey cried. "But I hope Freddie and Flossie are there!"

"Why don't we start calling to them?" Bert suggested.

"No, son, we'd better wait until we're ashore," his father cautioned. "They wouldn't be able to find us out here in the water."

At that moment the captain climbed back into the boat. "Not much harm done, praise be!" he said cheerfully. "We can fix up the crack with some pitch and tape from the shack that will do 'til we get back to the mainl'nd."

"What shack?" Bert asked. "Does someone live on this island?"

"No. But the Bankston fishermen keep supplies in a shack at the north beach. They have a small boat there, too, for fishing in the cove where their larger boats can't go."

"Is the cabin open?" asked Mrs. Bobbsey.

"Oh, yes, ma'am, but the fishermen are the only ones who come to this place," the captain replied.

"Then, if the balloon *did* come down on the island, the children might have found the shack and be there now, out of the rain and fog," Mrs. Bobbsey said hopefully.

"That's right," Captain North said. "I'll have the boys help you ashore now. Hank, you and Tom lend them a hand and get me some pitch and tape from the cabin."

The two men in short oilskin jackets sprang to help Mrs. Bobbsey and Nan over the side of the launch. Mr. Bobbsey, Bert, and the Carter brothers followed. They all went carefully over the slippery rocks and climbed to the shore.

"I'll have the *Nellie* waiting for you at the dock on the south shore," called Captain North. "That will be easier walking. Good luck. I hope you find the little ones safe."

The Bobbseys waved good-by to the friendly captain and hurried on their way. Before them through the heavy mist they could see what seemed to be a rough path, through the rank wet grass and trees. They followed it. Suddenly Nan stumbled and fell.

"It's a rope or something," she told Hank, who was the first to reach her. "It tripped me."

He bent and pulled a length of stiff, strong wire cable from the ground.

"That's one of the suspension wires from the balloon!" cried Alfred Carter. He began to scan the ground around them. "Here are more of them, twisted and broken. The basket must be around here somewhere!"

Bert's eyes followed the lengths of broken cable. He was the first to see the overturned basket. It lay on its side a few yards farther on.

"Glory be!" exclaimed Horace Carter, as he bent to examine it. "I do believe the basket isn't damaged at all."

"Well, the children couldn't have fallen far," remarked Mr. Bobbsey. "The basket must have spilled them out gently since it isn't broken."

"Here's an empty cracker box," called Nan. "And there's a water canteen over there."

Horace Carter gave a shout. "Here she is! Our old balloon is caught right up in this maple tree. Hank, can you give us a hand in getting it down?"

Bert began to shout out the small twins' names, cupping his hands about his mouth to make the sound carry farther.

"They probably picked themselves up and ran for shelter," observed Nan. "Could they see the cabin from here?" she asked Tom, the other boatman.

"No, ma'am, not in this soupy weather, but they might have taken cover in the woods over there. Then if they followed the trail through the trees they would have found the shack."

He pointed to their left toward a grove which they had not seen before.

"Is the shack far from here?" Nan asked.

"Yes," her mother added, "we want to find the children as soon as possible."

"I'm going over there now for the stuff to fix up *Nellie,*" Tom told her. "Follow me."

He led the way, and the Bobbseys followed him quickly. As they entered the grove Tom sniffed at its spicy fragrance. "This always reminds me of Christmas," he said. "It's all hemlock and pine around here, with a few undersized oaks and beeches on the south side."

"And lots of underbrush and shrubbery," observed Mr. Bobbsey, glancing around him.

Bert began to call out, "Freddie! Flossie! We're here! Where are you?"

There was no answer except the twitter of birds.

"They *must* be in the cabin," said Nan. "I'll bet they'll be glad to see us."

"They won't be any more glad than we will be to see *them!*" exclaimed Mrs. Bobbsey.

There was a crunching of pine needles under foot as Hank caught up with them. "We got the big balloon off the tree," he said. "And Horace Carter says he thinks it's in pretty good shape."

"That's very reassuring," said Mr. Bobbsey.

Mrs. Bobbsey stopped beside a glossy-leaved tangle of shrubbery. "Bert dear," she said,

Bert called out, "Freddie! Flossie! Where are you?"

"what's that yellow thing under the bushes?"

Bert reached under the shrubbery and came up with a small oilskin hat. "Hurray!" he shouted. "Now we know Freddie and Flossie are here!"

"That's Flossie's hat, all right," Mrs. Bobbsey said happily as she tucked it under her arm. "I wonder how she happened to lose it there."

Bert had gone back to the bushes. "I know. These are blueberry bushes, and there's hardly a ripe berry left on them. Flossie and Freddie must have had a feast."

"Poor little things!" Mrs. Bobbsey sighed. "They must be awfully hungry!"

"Well," the twins' father said as he stepped quickly along behind Tom, "we've practically found them now."

"They'll be waiting for you in the shack, for sure, ma'am," Hank assured Mrs. Bobbsey.

They all looked eagerly as they rounded a bend in the path and saw the cabin ahead. Bert called again, loud and strong. But no little figures came running out. With the Bobbseys close behind him, Tom strode over the grass and pushed open the door.

The cabin was empty.

"They're not here!" cried Mrs. Bobbsey, glancing about the single room in dismay. "Oh dear! Where can they be?"

"Not far away, I'm sure, Mary," answered her husband. "Freddie and Flossie are probably exploring the rest of the island."

"See what I found," Nan remarked, holding out her hand. In it was a red button.

"That's from Freddie's sweater," Mrs. Bobbsey cried. "At least we know the twins found the cabin!"

"Hank," said Tom, motioning him aside, "I don't see the rowboat. You carry the stuff back to the captain, and I'll take a look around the island. Someone may have left the boat on one of the other beaches, but then again those kids may be floundering in it somewhere on the lake!"

Hank, who was taking a large tin can from the shelf, replied, "All right. Keep a sharp eye out."

"I will," Tom promised as he disappeared into the fog.

Mr. Bobbsey had been studying the wall map. "We'll cover more ground if we separate," he proposed. "Bert, you and Nan take this end of the island, and your mother and I will cross to the other side."

"All right, Dad," Bert agreed. "We'll yell so Freddie and Flossie will hear us if they're anywhere near."

Both couples started off as Hank went back to

the *Nellie* with the mending supplies for Captain North. Bert and Nan called good-by to their parents and hurried across the beach by the shack. Mr. and Mrs. Bobbsey struck off through the woods to the southeast.

Bert called every few steps, but there was no response. "I think the fog muffles our voices," he said anxiously. "I wish it would lift. Flossie and Freddie probably can't hear me even if they *are* nearby."

"Won't they be surprised," said Nan, "to see us come out of the mist suddenly like magic?" She laughed, trying to keep up her spirits. "It will be fun to see the expressions on their faces."

Bert stopped and pointed ahead. "Here's another beach. It goes up around the eastern end of the island. See? We cut right across through the woods." As he spoke he looked in both directions.

Nan nodded. She could not keep back a discouraged sigh. "I hope Mother and Dad are having more luck than we are. Oh, Bert, where *can* Freddie and Flossie be?"

Bert did not reply immediately. He was staring across the white-shrouded water. Finally he turned to say slowly, "Nan, I believe they took that rowboat. I overheard Tom tell Hank it was missing. The boat isn't anywhere on this beach, either. It would be just like Freddie. He thinks he's a whale of a rower."

"Oh, they couldn't take a boat out by themselves," protested his sister. "They're too little."

"Never underestimate the younger Bobbsey twins," Bert told her. "They'll attempt anything."

Nan bit her lip anxiously. "And we thought we were about to find them safe and sound! It's frightening to think of them out in a boat. Do you really think they could manage to row it?"

Bert nodded. "I'm more and more sure of it. Ever since that day of our picnic at Pine Grove, Freddie has been wanting a chance to row again. He did very well, too, but even *I* wouldn't want to take a boat out in this pea soup."

He turned quickly and ran to the edge of the water to shout at the top of his lungs. Nan sat down on a log, thinking hard. She felt very sad. Nevertheless she racked her brain to figure out what they should do next.

Bert continued to call Freddie and Flossie as he walked on. Soon he was out of sight around the point of land. Nan could hear his voice shouting in the distance.

A crackling in the underbrush behind her brought the girl to her feet. She whirled about, hoping it would be her father and mother with news of success.

Instead of their familiar faces, Nan saw the ungainly hulk of a brown bear!

CHAPTER XIV

A MYSTERY

AS NAN stared at the bear, her heart almost stopped from fright. The animal came toward her, giving short grunts as he lumbered up.

Suddenly Nan remembered the bag of candy she had bought that morning at the fair. It was still in her pocket. "I've always heard that bears like sweets," she thought. "I hope this one does!"

Timidly she tossed a piece of chocolate in the direction of the oncoming beast. To her delight the bear stopped, sniffed the candy, then sat back on his haunches and put it in his mouth. When he had finished the candy he gave an approving grunt and ambled toward the girl.

She waited until he had almost reached her, then quickly threw another chocolate. The animal flopped down again to enjoy the sweet.

After Nan had given him several more pieces,

The bear sat back on his haunches

she thought desperately, "I haven't much more candy. I hope someone comes soon!"

Just as she was flinging the last chocolate, she heard a man's voice from the woods. "Teddy! Teddy! Come get your honey."

It was Hank! He appeared from the undergrowth carrying a large tin can. At sight of him, the bear lumbered over to the fisherman. Hank took a large scoop of honey from the can and dribbled it into the bear's mouth.

Nan sank down weakly on the log. "Do you know this bear?" she asked in amazement.

Hank laughed and fed the bear another scoop of honey. "Oh, yes. I'm sorry he frightened you. He's been a pet of the fishermen in Bankston since he was a cub. We keep honey in the shack just for him."

"Well," Nan said, "he looks awfully scary if you don't know him! Would he hurt little children?"

"Shucks, no," Hank replied. "He loves to play with kids."

"I gave him all my candy, and he wanted more," Nan explained. "What would he have done if you hadn't come along?"

"I reckon he'd have pestered you until you went to the cabin and got him something else to eat," Hank said with a grin.

"I wonder if the twins saw him," Nan said with a worried look.

"Maybe so," Hank mused. "Perhaps he scared them so they took the rowboat and shoved off." Then he laughed. "All right, Teddy. Take the whole can. There's not much left anyway!"

Teddy took the tin in his paws and went off into the woods to finish the honey.

"Nan! Nan!" Bert called as he came running along the shore. "I heard the twins! They're out on the water somewhere!"

Nan raced across the sand to follow Bert, who had turned about and was flying up the beach again. Hank ran behind her.

"Freddie! Flossie! Where are you?" shouted Bert.

Then Freddie's voice came clearly out of the fog. "We're coming!"

There was the sound of oars dipping, and then Hank gave a shout. "There they are. They're almost in."

He leaped into the water beside Bert, and together they brought the rowboat up onto the sand. Nan hugged the weary, bedraggled children as she led them up onto the beach.

Flossie clung to her big sister. "Oh, Nan, we were all lost and mixed up. The old horn kept blowing, but we couldn't see it."

Hank chuckled. "It's the foghorn over on Harvey's Point, she means."

He patted Flossie on the shoulder. "I'm glad you're back on dry land. I'll take the boat back to the other side. I think we'll need it to carry the balloon stuff over to Bankston."

He left them and pushed off in the boat. The four Bobbsey twins went joyfully across the beach.

"Freddie's an awfully good rower," Flossie said proudly. "He rowed for hours and hours."

Bert patted his little brother on the shoulder. "It sure must have seemed like that, Freddie. I don't see how you could've gotten anywhere in that fog."

"I didn't," Freddie answered. "I guess I must have been going round and round instead of straight ahead."

Flossie added, "I thought we were way over near the other shore."

"Where's Billy?" Freddie asked.

"Billy?" asked Bert. "He isn't with us."

"But we heard him," Flossie protested.

"Oh, you heard Bert," said Nan. "The fog may have made his voice sound like Billy's."

"But he answered us, didn't he, Flossie?" Freddie insisted, and Flossie nodded.

"We said, 'Where are you?' and he said,

'On the island,' " the little girl explained.

"It couldn't have been Billy," Nan told her. "We heard the calliope when we left the fair grounds."

Just then Flossie screamed. They had reached the edge of the woods where Teddy was sitting with his nose deep in the honey tin. Flossie threw her arms around Nan, and Freddie took Bert's hand tightly.

Nan was glad that she could say calmly, "Oh, that's just Teddy. He's the fishermen's pet, and he won't hurt you."

Freddie peered around Bert's protecting arm to look at Nan. "Who told you that, Nan? That bear chased us into the cabin!"

"That fellow named Hank told me about the bear," Nan said. "Fishermen found him when he was a cub and have kept him on the island as a pet. They store honey in the cabin for him. He probably thought you and Flossie were going to the cabin to get him some."

Flossie still did not feel entirely reassured. She cast a dubious glance at the brown bear and pulled at Nan's hand. "Let's go away from here while he's eating his honey," she urged.

"That's a good idea, Floss," Bert agreed as he started on with Freddie. "Let eating bears eat!" he teased.

The sight of the bear temporarily had driven all thoughts about Billy Fagan from the little twins' minds.

"Where are Mother and Daddy?" asked Flossie eagerly as the four children hurried quickly past the bear and followed the path through the woods.

"Searching for you on the other side of the island," Bert replied. "They are probably on their way back now."

He and Nan quickly told Flossie and Freddie the details of the trip aboard the *Nellie* to Hemlock Island. "Oh boy!" Freddie exclaimed when he heard of the fishing launch's rocky landing. "We all had bumpy rides today."

Flossie gave a little shiver. "I'd rather be bumped in a boat than a balloon," she stated.

At that moment Mr. and Mrs. Bobbsey appeared around a bend in the path. Mrs. Bobbsey saw them first. "Oh!" she cried out. "Thank goodness! Here they are! Nan and Bert have found them!"

The small twins, hugged over and over by their parents, tried to tell everything at once.

"We were 'most tipped over into the water out of the balloon," began Flossie.

"But you weren't," their father laughed.

"You were spilled out gently on a bed of wet leaves."

"How did you know, Daddy?" Freddie asked in surprise.

"We found the basket, and it wasn't damaged at all, so we were pretty sure you two weren't hurt either," his father told him.

"Well, anyway, a great big bear chased us," Flossie went on, "and Freddie rowed us away in a boat and it was all foggy."

"Whoa!" exclaimed Mr. Bobbsey. "You're going too fast for me. A big bear? A boat?"

"I think we'd better hear this adventure on the way back to the *Nellie*," Mrs. Bobbsey put in. "Captain North is waiting for us at the dock on the south beach."

The united Bobbsey family went single file along the path through the woods. Mr. Bobbsey and Freddie were the last in line. Suddenly Mr. Bobbsey stopped. "There's someone behind us," he said. "Who could it be?"

He and Freddie turned and waited. A moment later Teddy, the brown bear, lumbered into view around a bend in the path.

"Hurry, Freddie!" Mr. Bobbsey exclaimed. "We must—"

Freddie stood still and said manfully, "That's

Teddy, Daddy. He's the fishermen's pet. He won't hurt us."

To Mr. Bobbsey's utter amazement the bear ambled off through the woods in the opposite direction.

As all the Bobbseys continued through the woods, Mr. and Mrs. Bobbsey were told of the small twins' first encounter with Teddy, and then Nan's.

"Gracious!" Mrs. Bobbsey cried. And when Flossie and Freddie described their rowboat ride, Mr. Bobbsey shook his head. "You've certainly had adventure by land, water, and air today!" he exclaimed.

Finally the family crossed the south beach toward the small wharf where the *Nellie* was tied up.

Captain North saw them coming and called out, "Welcome back, little Bobbsey travelers!"

The two Carter brothers and Hank had folded the bag of the balloon into a large flat package and were tying it. As soon as it was secure they came to greet the Bobbseys.

"Congratulations on your safe landing," Alfred Carter said to the younger twins.

Mr. Bobbsey introduced Freddie and Flossie to the Carters and to Captain North and the other seamen.

"How did you like the balloon flight, Freddie?" Alfred Carter asked.

"If we hadn't been so scared it would have been fun," the little boy answered.

"Well, you're both celebrities now. I'm pretty sure you're the only children who've made an ascent alone in a balloon," said Horace.

Captain North shook hands with Flossie and Freddie. "I think you've been very brave," he said. "Now we'll head back to Bankston."

As they walked aboard the launch Horace Carter asked Freddie and Flossie, "Would you like to go up in the balloon again if we went with you?"

Freddie's eyes brightened. He remembered the feeling of sailing high in the air. "I think I'd like it if you were there," he answered.

Flossie shook her head firmly. "No, thank you. I'd rather not go in a balloon again—ever!" she told him.

"Will you be able to make other ascents with this balloon?" Mr. Bobbsey asked Alfred Carter.

"I think so," the owner answered cheerfully. "There are ways of re-enforcing this material so that the gas bag can be as strong as before. There was no actual break in it which means the bag must have deflated before it landed on the tree."

"How thankful we all should be!" Mrs. Bobbsey exclaimed, putting an arm around each of the two small adventurers.

As the *Nellie* pulled away from the dock, Captain North called, "Look! The fog has lifted!"

Nan glanced back at the dark woods on Hemlock Island and then at the dancing, sunlit ripples of the water before her.

"The sun is out at last," she cried happily. "What a lovely ending to this worrisome day!"

Flossie was not paying attention. She gazed at the island, wrinkling her forehead. She had remembered hearing Billy Fagan's voice calling to her and Freddie from among the trees.

"Oh dear!" she thought. "What if Billy ran away again and is on Hemlock Island all alone!"

CHAPTER XV

STOWAWAY!

SOON Hemlock Island was left behind. The trip back to Bankston on the *Nellie* was very different from the one going out. The heavy fog had completely lifted, and the sky was a cloudless blue.

Freddie and Flossie were safe, and everyone was in gay spirits—everyone but Flossie. She kept thinking of Billy. Had her imagination been playing tricks on her?

"What's on your mind, little daydreamer?" Nan teased her as the four twins sat perched on the low roof of the launch cabin.

"Oh—nothing," Flossie answered hastily.

Captain North listened with keen interest to the full story of the small twins' balloon flight and experiences on the island.

"You are real adventurers!" he exclaimed. "Ready for anything!"

"We knew that Daddy would come for us," Flossie told him, smiling at her father. "I just hoped there weren't any cannibals around."

"I'm most hungry enough to be a cannibal," Bert remarked, pretending to nibble at Flossie's ear. "I think I'll eat you."

"I'm hungry, too," Freddie moaned. "I've been hungry for ages."

"I'll get some ship's biscuits," offered Captain North. "They're not very fresh, but at least they'll keep you from starvation until you can get something more." He asked Hank to take the wheel and disappeared into the cabin.

"Is there a restaurant in Bankston where our ravenous family can eat at this time of day?" Mr. Bobbsey asked one of the balloon owners.

"The hotel serves meals in the coffee shop any time," Horace Carter told him. "The food is good, too," he added.

Alfred Carter nodded. "Horace and I would like to take everyone there as our guests."

Mr. Bobbsey protested. "I had planned to ask you all to be my guests. I insist."

Just then the captain came up out of the cabin. "Look what I found!" he said. "A stowaway!"

Behind him was Billy Fagan.

"Look what I found!" he said. "A stowaway!"

Before Captain North could tell anything else the Bobbseys were clustered around Billy and all talking at once.

"Oh, Billy!" Nan exclaimed. "You're soaking wet."

The lad's clothes were indeed drenched, and he stood shivering.

"I *knew* I heard you on the island!" Flossie declared.

"Have you run away again, Billy?" Freddie asked. "And didn't you call to Flossie and me from Hemlock Island?"

Billy nodded. He looked as if he were about to cry.

"Whatever are you doing here?" Hank asked.

"Now hold on," said the captain. "Give the lad a chance. You Bobbseys know this boy?"

"Yes," chorused the twins.

"Indeed we do," said Mr. Bobbsey. "He plays a mighty fine calliope at the Bolton fair." Mr. Bobbsey smiled to reassure the boy. Billy was still shivering in his wet clothes, and the captain brought out a woolen blanket and put it around him.

Billy thanked him, then began to apologize to the captain. "I'm sorry I stowed away on your boat, sir. But I had to get off that island. There was a bear—"

At this point Freddie and Flossie giggled, and Nan told Billy about the twins' adventures with Teddy.

"I don't mind your stowing away." Captain North laughed. "But it's a mighty uncomfortable ride down below where you were. I wish you'd just asked. I'm glad to have you aboard."

"I was afraid," confessed Billy. "The bear, I mean Teddy, chased me into the water, and after I swam around awhile, I saw your boat. No one seemed to be on it. I just climbed in. Then when I heard someone, I hid for fear you'd throw me off."

"What! Throw anyone off the *Nellie?*" asked the captain good-naturedly. "Why, *Nellie* wouldn't approve of that, no, sir."

"But how did you get on the island in the first place?" Hank wanted to know.

"Yes, Billy," said Mrs. Bobbsey. "Tell us your story. Have you left Ben Fagan again?"

Billy nodded and Mr. Bobbsey asked, "Has he been mistreating you again?"

"Well—" Billy replied hesitatingly. "I—I'd really rather not talk about it yet."

"Of course," said Mrs. Bobbsey. "You've been through a very disturbing day. You can tell us all about it when you feel better."

Billy smiled gratefully at Mrs. Bobbsey, then

turned to the twins. "You've certainly had lots of excitement," he ventured. "I heard about your balloon ride."

"Did you see us go up?" Freddie asked eagerly.

"No, I didn't," Billy admitted. "I was playing the calliope. But it was all over the fair grounds that some children had been in the balloon when it broke loose. I ran over to the station as soon as I could and found out that it was Freddie and Flossie."

"I'll bet you were surprised," Freddie declared.

"I certainly was," agreed Billy. "I'm sure glad you were rescued safely."

"We're glad you were, too," chimed in Flossie.

By now Billy's clothes were almost dried out by the blanket and heat of the sun. He had stopped shivering. The boy said he would put the blanket inside the cabin.

He went to do this and returned with a bundle which he handed to Bert.

"I didn't have a chance to return this earlier. I'm afraid it's a little wet now," he said, as Bert unwrapped the sweater he had lent to Billy. "I brought it along, hoping I'd meet you so I could give it back."

"Where are you going, Billy?" Nan asked in concern.

"I don't exactly know where I'll go—"

"Nonsense!" exclaimed Mr. Bobbsey. "You'll come with us."

Billy started to protest, but he was too tired and hungry to refuse when Mrs. Bobbsey said, "At least you must have something to eat with us."

The twins were very pleased to have Billy as their guest, and Mr. Bobbsey said, "Of course we'd like you and your crew to join us, Captain North."

"Well, that's mighty nice of you," said the captain, thanking Mr. Bobbsey, "but we've got a lot of fishing to do before sundown, so I guess we'll have to head back out right away."

The *Nellie* was making good time, and the town of Bankston lay just ahead of them. Many small boats were in the tiny harbor, and their sails looked very gay. As the launch pulled up to the wharf, Mr. Bobbsey said to the captain:

"This is a mission well done, Captain North. I can't tell you how much we appreciate your help."

Mrs. Bobbsey added her heartfelt thanks, saying, "The *Nellie* will always have a special place in the hearts of the Bobbsey family."

The captain beamed at these words and refused the money Mr. Bobbsey tried to press into his hand. "You have a fine family, sir." He smiled at the twins. "I've had ample payment in seeing these two youngsters return safe and sound." The captain of the *Nellie* patted Flossie and Freddie on the head.

Flossie looked up at him. "Thank you for a nice boat ride," she said.

"And I hope you catch lots of fish," Freddie added.

Then the Bobbseys, Billy, and the Carter brothers said good-by to the *Nellie* and her crew and went ashore. They headed at once for the Bankston hotel.

As they sat at a table in the hotel coffee shop, Horace Carter said to Mr. Bobbsey, "This adventure of the twins may turn out to be very good advertisement for our balloon."

"Yes," agreed Mr. Bobbsey enthusiastically. "The happy landing will prove how sturdily it's built."

"There will probably be some publicity for the children. I hope you won't mind," said Alfred Carter.

"What's publicity, Nan?" Flossie whispered.

"Mr. Carter means that everyone will hear about your balloon ride," Nan whispered back.

Mr. Bobbsey answered after a thoughtful silence, "I suppose there's bound to be some notice taken of such an unusual event, but we really don't like publicity."

Alfred Carter smiled. "I understand how you feel, Mr. Bobbsey. After the first story of their flight we won't mention the twins' names again. But I'd like to take Freddie up some time when he can enjoy the ride and not have any worries."

Mrs. Bobbsey thanked him. "We're going home in a day or two," she said. "But perhaps sometime Freddie will take you up on that offer."

After a satisfying meal, the Bobbseys and Billy bade the Carter brothers good-by and were soon on their way to Meadowbrook. There was a great shout from the doorway as they drove into the yard. Aunt Sarah, Uncle Daniel, and Harry came running out to hug the small twins. They were delighted to see Billy with them.

Mr. Bobbsey and his brother went off by themselves to discuss the boy's case. They decided to phone the lawyer and ask his advice in the matter.

In the meantime the twins and Billy went to change their clothes. Harry gave him a pair of dungarees and a shirt to put on. A little later everyone gathered in the living room.

"Billy," said Nan, "do you feel like telling us how you beat all of us to the island?"

"Of course," the runaway replied. His spirits had risen considerably.

"Why don't you start at the beginning?" Bert suggested.

"Well." Billy drew a deep breath and began. "This morning I was in Ben Fagan's tent, and I saw Bert's missing camera. I knew it was his because of the initials on the case. But just then Ben came in, and he was furious when he saw that I knew about the stolen property. He—he hit me and warned me to keep my mouth shut about it—or else."

"How dreadful!" Nan exclaimed.

"That awful man!" Flossie cried out.

"Go on, Billy," Mr. Bobbsey said quietly.

"Later on I saw Ben packing his things. He didn't say anything to Mr. Bates or me, but I'm sure he was planning to leave. I think he's in some kind of trouble. Sometimes he disappears for hours at a time and never says where he's been.

"After you Bobbseys left the merry-go-round," Billy continued, "Ben came over and said he wanted to see me after the next ride. He ordered me to meet him at one of the concessions. I decided then to run away, because I was afraid he was going to leave Mr. Bates and make me go some place else with him. So as soon as I had a chance I dashed back to the tent, grabbed my things, and took off.

"On the road some people picked me up in their car and gave me a ride to Bankston. Then I went down to the docks and heard some fisher-men say they were going out past Hemlock Is-land. I thought if I could get there, Ben Fagan never would find me, so I hid on the fishing boat. When we got near the island I slid into the wa-ter and swam the rest of the way to shore.

"I wandered around for a while, and when I got to the beach I heard Freddie yelling. I re-membered about the balloon and realized he and Flossie must have landed near the island. I called back, thinking I could help them.

"Just then I saw Bert, and knew Flossie and Freddie would be all right. You Bobbseys have done so much for me, I—I didn't want to make any more trouble for you. So I hid, but Teddy the bear came along." Billy smiled in recollec-tion. "The rest you know about."

"Whew!" Bert whistled. "That's some adven-ture! We want you to stay here until we find out what Ben Fagan's up to."

"Now, Dad," Harry said, "tell them *your* ex-citing news."

CHAPTER XVI

A LITTLE HERO

"WONDERFUL!" exclaimed Nan. "What is your exciting news, Uncle Daniel?"

She and the rest of her family looked at him expectantly.

"This morning seems a long time ago," the twins' uncle began. "What a lot has happened since Harry and I went to see about our sheep at the fair grounds!"

"Were the little lambs all right?" Flossie asked anxiously.

"Yes, indeed," Uncle Daniel replied. "They're being very well taken care of over there. Well, as Harry and I were leaving the exhibition tent, we met a friend of mine who always serves as one of the judges at the race track.

"I remembered something of Freddie's story," he continued, "so I asked Allen Kirk, my friend, which horse had won last night. He said that the best two-year-old in Manley stables was the winner of the big race. His name is White Star."

"Whoopee!" cried Freddie. "I knew he would! The van driver on the way to Meadowbrook said he was the best, and that I'd bring him good luck. Remember?"

"You brought White Star better luck than that," Uncle Daniel remarked. "Mr. Kirk told me that a rival jockey named Tony Lenaro had tried to injure White Star and put him out of the running before that race. The horse made such a racket that some of the stablemen went running in to see what was the matter. They found Lenaro on the floor in a bad state of fright. He was babbling something about a snake jumping out at him from under the horse."

The Bobbseys burst into laughter, and Billy looked on wide-eyed.

Uncle Daniel went on, "The stablemen thought the jockey was crazy and carted him off to question him. But afterward they found one of those whistles that shoot out at you—but that is getting ahead of my story."

"Oh, ho ho, he thought it was a snake!" Freddie doubled up with laughter.

"Please go on," Bert urged his uncle.

"White Star's jockey came running in just as

they were taking this fellow out. He saw a big wrench in Lenaro's hand and knew he had been trying to lame the horse who was sure to win the race. White Star's jockey was so excited that he didn't think of anything else.

"It seems that just about then a certain small boy came around from behind the horse. He said something to the jockey about hoping he hadn't scared White Star too much, and that he had blown the whistle to scare the bad man. But the jockey was only half listening and hustled the boy out of the stables."

"He sure did," Freddie spoke up, grinning at the recollection.

Billy stared at him. "You mean *you* were the boy who blew the snake whistle?"

Uncle Daniel smiled. "You've guessed it." Then he went on with his story.

"The jockey took Freddie out to the gate keeper. But later, after the jockey had calmed down, he began to think about what the boy had said. Then one of the stablemen came in and told him Tony Lenaro kept insisting that a snake had jumped out from under the horse. The jockey remembered Freddie's showing him the snake-whistle. So the men looked all around the straw-covered floor and found the whistle still there."

Uncle Daniel laughed. "I was told the jockey said excitedly, 'Galloping grasshoppers! That kid did tell me he blew his whistle to scare Lenaro so he wouldn't hurt White Star!' The jockey went running out to find the boy, but he'd gone and no one knew his name."

Uncle Daniel paused, then said, "So I told him!"

Flossie suddenly gave Freddie a tight hug. "You're a hero!" she exclaimed.

The others laughed, and Mrs. Bobbsey said proudly, "Yes, Freddie certainly is a hero."

"I haven't quite finished my story," Uncle Daniel said. "When they questioned the bad jockey later, he said he'd been hired to hurt White Star, but, even though Lenaro had been jailed, he wouldn't tell who had paid him the money."

"Oh, I know!" cried Freddie.

Uncle Daniel held up a finger and smiled at the little boy. "Then I remembered what Freddie had said yesterday at lunch about having seen Ben Fagan behind the stable giving money to a man in a green jacket. I told Kirk about that, too."

Just then the telephone rang, and Aunt Sarah answered it. "For you, Dick," she said to the twins' father.

Bert turned to Billy. "It sounds like Ben Fagan was mixed up in trying to fix that race."

Billy nodded as Mr. Bobbsey returned, and Uncle Daniel continued his story. "Mr. Kirk reported what I told him to the stable managers this morning, and later White Star's owner, Mr. Manley, telephoned that Lenaro finally confessed today that it was Ben Fagan who bribed him to injure White Star."

The twins' uncle explained that Mr. Fagan had staked a great deal of money on another horse to win before knowing that White Star had been entered in the race.

"Fagan knew his horse had no chance against White Star," he added.

"You mean that terrible man wanted to hurt that poor horse just to try saving his money!" Nan exclaimed, shocked.

"I'm afraid that is exactly what Ben Fagan meant to do," Uncle Daniel said. Then he smiled. "Mr. Manley told me something else. He wants to meet the boy who saved his horse from injury."

"Me?" Freddie asked.

"Who else?" Harry teased.

Freddie was pleased, though somewhat awed at the thought of meeting White Star's owner.

"When will I see Mr. Manley?" he wanted to know.

"I told Mr. Kirk," his uncle replied, "that we all would be at the fair grounds tomorrow, and that we'd meet Mr. Manley there."

At that moment Aunt Sarah announced that supper was ready. Everyone went into the dining room. Aunt Sarah said with a twinkle, "Billy, you sit between Harry and me and keep us from misbehaving."

The boys grinned and took their places at the table.

"Blueberry muffins!" Nan exclaimed. "Oh, Aunt Sarah, you know how I love them!"

"I hope there are acres of them," said Freddie. "I'm hungry again!"

"Acres of blueberries or muffins?" Bert teased.

"What adventures you twins have had!" Aunt Sarah remarked after grace had been said. "You have crowded more thrills into two days than we have in a year!"

Harry laughed and remarked, "That's one reason it's such fun to have my cousins from Lakeport come to visit us. There's always excitement."

Mrs. Bobbsey watched Billy Fagan as he looked around the table at the happy faces. How wonderful it would be, she thought, if Billy could belong to a family like this one! Billy saw Mrs. Bobbsey smiling at him. He smiled back.

"Billy," Mr. Bobbsey leaned forward, "you're to stay here for the night. I want to take you to see a man who is a lawyer. He lives a little way from here. He just phoned me to say that the adoption paper Ben Fagan has is an absolute fake!"

"What!" Bert cried out. "Then Billy doesn't belong to Mr. Fagan!"

Everyone was amazed at the news, and delighted besides. A look of utter astonishment on Billy's face was followed by one of relief.

"How did you find out, sir?" he asked.

"Mr. Gardner, the lawyer, wired the court down South. The reply was that there had never been such an adoption," Mr. Bobbsey explained. "Ben Fagan is a dishonest schemer, Billy, and I see no reason for your staying with that outfit of his."

"Such wonderful news!" Nan exclaimed.

Mr. Bobbsey and his brother explained that they had not wished to raise any false hopes. For this reason they had said nothing about their first discussion with the lawyer.

"We decided to wait until Mr. Gardner carried out his investigation," Mr. Bobbsey said.

Billy set his jaw. "I never want to see Ben Fagan again," he asserted.

Uncle Daniel now joined in. "You must stay here with us until it's decided by the court what you should do."

"But who will play the calliope?" Billy asked.

"You're not to worry about that," Mr. Bobbsey assured him. "Ben Fagan will have to find someone else to play it, when and if he ever resumes business. He'll be in a lot of trouble when the law catches up with him."

Billy was so overcome with joy that he could not find words to thank his new friends. While he was trying to express what he felt, a bell chimed.

"The front door!" said Uncle Daniel and went to answer it.

Billy turned pale and said fearfully, "I—I hope that's not Ben Fagan!"

"I doubt it," Mrs. Bobbsey calmed him.

The group at the table, who had just finished their supper, heard a man's voice from the front hall saying, "Where are the little twins who had a ride in a runaway balloon? We want to interview them and take some pictures for the paper."

CHAPTER XVII

A THRILLING CHASE

WHEN Bert heard the reporter asking for the twins who had been in the runaway balloon, he whistled. "Jeepers! Freddie and Flossie are really famous now!" he said.

Uncle Daniel returned to the dining room. "The newspapermen want to take pictures as well as talk to the children," he said.

Mrs. Bobbsey went with the small twins into the living room where the photographer and the reporter were waiting. "I hope this won't take too long," she said with a smile. "The children have had a full day and should get to bed soon."

"We'll make it quick," the reporter promised. "The pictures can be snapped while we're talking."

The flash bulbs went off as Freddie and Flossie related their adventure and answered the reporter's questions. Finally he closed his notebook and said, "Thank you very much, Freddie and Flossie. Watch for the story in the *Bolton News*."

The small twins smiled sleepily, and after saying good-by to the newspapermen, went to kiss their father and say good night to the others. Then they followed their mother upstairs. A short time later, after she came down, Uncle Daniel turned to Billy and said:

"I'd like you to meet Mr. John Gardner tonight. He's a fine lawyer, and I think he'd be interested in hearing your story as soon as possible."

"That's a good idea, Daniel," the twins' father said. "Let's go now."

Billy eagerly jumped up to join the two men. Bert, Nan, and Harry asked if they might go along.

Mr. Bobbsey smiled as he noticed Bert try to stifle an immense yawn. "I think," he said, "you three had better stay here and go to bed. We'll tell you what happened tomorrow."

Although disappointed, the children had to admit they were getting drowsy. Bert grinned. "I hope you won't mind, Billy, if Harry and I aren't awake when you come back."

"Of course not," Billy replied. Then he turned

to Aunt Sarah and added, "It's wonderful of you to let me stay here tonight."

"We're mighty glad to have you, Billy," she answered sincerely. "And I think you'll like Mr. Gardner."

After he and the men had gone Nan immediately said good night and went to bed.

The two boys retired soon afterward and were half asleep when Billy returned an hour or so later. Bert heard him whistling softly as he undressed, but was too sleepy to speak. He was glad that his friend was so happy.

The next morning Billy told the boys that Mr. Gardner was going to the fair with him and the Bobbseys that day. "Mr. Gardner is almost as wonderful as you folks," he added.

After breakfast the lawyer's car pulled into the driveway. The Bobbseys and their young guest hurried outside.

Mr. Bobbsey and Uncle Daniel introduced their families to Mr. Gardner, who was tall and had twinkling brown eyes. After everyone exchanged greetings, Billy climbed in next to Mr. Gardner, and the rest piled into the two station wagons. When the three cars reached the fair grounds, the men and Billy led the way to the merry-go-round concession.

Upon the group's arrival they saw another man coming from Ben Fagan's tent. The twins recognized him as Mr. Sheldon, the detective, who had come with Ben Fagan when Billy had first run away. He nodded to them, then announced grimly: "Looks like Fagan has skipped. His tent is empty."

"And I don't see Mr. Bates anywhere," Mr. Bobbsey frowned. "I might have known that scoundrel Fagan would disappear before I brought a lawyer to see him."

Just then Alonzo Bates came running up to them. He seemed glad to see Detective Sheldon.

"My partner has run off with all our money!" he cried. "Besides taking the cash we had, Ben went and drew out the money we had in the bank over in Long Branch day before yesterday. Billy has disappeared, too," he finished glumly.

"Billy is with us," Mr. Bobbsey said quickly, and the boy stepped up to speak to Mr. Bates.

"I should have let you know where I was," he said. "But I was afraid Mr. Fagan would find out."

"He was plenty mad when you didn't show up yesterday," Alonzo Bates said. "He got a man in who played an accordion for the afternoon and evening. Then some time after midnight the old cheat ran off with the money."

"He's worse than a cheat, Mr. Bates," the twins' father spoke up. "Ben Fagan had the adoption papers for Billy faked. Also, he tried to fix the race here the other night."

Alonzo Bates looked stunned. Then he said sadly, "I knew Ben could be very mean, but I sure never realized he was an out-and-out crook!"

Mr. Bates turned to Billy. "You come back with me, boy. Now that Ben has gone, we can make a *good* thing of this business."

Before Billy could reply, Mr. Bobbsey put a hand on the boy's shoulder, saying, "We have other plans for Billy now, Mr. Bates. He deserves a good education and opportunity for a better life."

Bert and Nan exchanged glances. What did their father mean?

Mr. Bates nodded understandingly. "I'm glad he has found friends."

The detective began to question Mr. Bates about Ben Fagan, and soon a description of the missing man was broadcast over the area.

Billy felt sorry for Mr. Bates. "I'll stay and play the calliope this morning for the merry-go-round," he offered.

By now it was time for Freddie to meet Mr. Manley at the stables, so his parents and aunt and uncle went with him. Bert, Harry, Nan, and Flossie wanted to ride on the merry-go-round. The lawyer and detective said they would rejoin the group at the Ferris wheel around noon.

The gay notes of the wheezy calliope brought crowds of children, and the merry-go-round did a fine business that morning. Mr. Bates left Bert in charge of tickets while he went to arrange for the accordion player to take Billy's place later on.

"This is fun," said Bert. "Two tickets, madam?" he repeated to a woman who had come up with two small children.

"Is it safe?" she asked worriedly.

"Oh, yes," Harry answered with a grin. "Our lions and tigers never bite, and our horses never buck!"

Near noontime the boys and girls left the merry-go-round to go to the Ferris wheel. On the way they met Mr. Gardner and Detective Sheldon, who were coming to speak to Mr. Bates.

The lawyer stopped to say softly, "There's a good chance that Ben Fagan may be somewhere on the grounds. We have reason to think he has a friend who may be hiding him. Be on your guard, Billy. He might try to harm you in some way."

"We'll stay close to Billy," Bert assured him. "Just let him try something!"

Mr. Gardner smiled. "I'll meet you at the dining tent in half an hour," he called, as he left them.

The children found their parents and Freddie waiting for them at the Ferris wheel. The little boy's eyes were shining with excitement and happiness.

"What did Mr. Manley say to you, Freddie?" Nan asked at once.

"He thanked me for scaring the bad man, and I had my picture taken with White Star and he's going to frame it." Freddie stopped to take a deep breath, then went on. "He wanted to give me a pony, but Daddy said we had no place to keep it, so he said that whenever I wanted to ride I could come to his farm and use any pony I want to!"

"Wow!" breathed Bert. "Does that go for the rest of the family, too?"

"I guess it does." Freddie grinned. Then they all set out for the dining tent. Mr. Gardner joined them as they entered.

There were people waiting, but before long a waiter pushed two tables together for the Bobbsey party. As they were sitting down, Mr. Gardner said, "There's Tom Sheldon. Let's make room for him, too." He hailed the detective, who had just come into the tent.

Bert noticed that the waiter who laid a place for the newcomer was much older than the first one. He had bushy gray hair and a mustache which was so large it almost hid his face.

They gave their orders, and Uncle Daniel, who was seated beside the detective, asked him, "What luck have you had this morning, Mr. Sheldon? Anything new on Ben Fagan's disappearance?"

Tom Sheldon grinned but said only, "Well, no, but I'm playing a hunch, Mr. Bobbsey."

Uncle Daniel laughed. "Well, I guess it's better not to talk about it here," he said.

Bert, sitting across from the two men, noticed that the elderly waiter seemed to be listening to them. When the man saw that Bert was watching him he hastened to take Aunt Sarah's order.

Freddie was telling Harry more about his meeting with Mr. Manley that morning when the waiters returned with the luncheon orders. "He was awful glad that White Star didn't get hurt," the little boy related, "and he said—"

"Look out!" cried Bert, as the tray carried by the elderly waiter tipped dangerously toward Freddie.

Nan had seen the tilting tray, too, and snatched

Freddie out of the way just in time to save him
from being burned by the hot soup. The other
waiter hurriedly brought a cloth to remove the
spilled soup, scolding the old man for his care-
lessness.

"It's all right," said Mrs. Bobbsey, feeling
sorry for the man. "No one was hurt."

Bert looked sharply at the clumsy waiter but
said nothing.

The others were served. Then the elderly
waiter came to put Bert's plate before him. As

he bent over, Bert reached up suddenly and snatched at the waiter's big gray mustache.

It came off in Bert's hand, and the amazed people at the table saw before them the ugly red face of Ben Fagan. His eyes glared with anger below the gray wig. Then he dropped the plate and ran!

"Get him!" shouted Detective Sheldon.

CHAPTER XVIII

BILLY FINDS A HOME

WHEN Ben Fagan realized that he had been discovered, he bolted from the Bobbseys' table, knocking chairs and patrons aside as he ran.

Bert and Detective Sheldon were the first on their feet to dash after the fugitive. Fagan disappeared between the folds of the adjoining tent which served as a kitchen, leaving confusion behind him.

"Where is he! Where did he go?" Tom shouted as he and Bert burst into the kitchen tent. There was no sign of the impostor.

The chief cook in his white cap was standing by the stove with a startled expression on his face. "If you mean the new waiter, he ran out that way." The chef pointed to a flap in the tent beyond an overturned table. "What's the matter with that fellow anyway?" he asked. "Are spooks after him?"

171

Bert and the detective did not take time to answer. They dashed outside, then stopped to look around. They saw no one who resembled Ben Fagan in the milling crowd.

"Any sign of him?" Mr. Bobbsey gasped as he, Mr. Gardner, Harry, Billy, and Nan came rushing out of the refreshment tent to join them.

"Not a chance!" Detective Sheldon groaned. "He's lost himself in this mass of people."

"Well, anyway, he's probably somewhere on the fair grounds," Bert remarked.

"That's right," the detective agreed. "Our job now is to find him. We'd better spread out and each go in a different direction. Look carefully at everyone you pass. Fagan may try another disguise."

Everyone agreed, and Bert ran into the tent to tell his mother of the plan.

"Be careful," Mrs. Bobbsey said. "Aunt Sarah and I will wait here with Freddie and Flossie."

The boy nodded and dashed back outside. The group of searchers separated, after arranging to meet back at the dining tent in an hour to report.

Nan, Billy, and the detective chose a side lane and walked along slowly, searching for a clue to Ben Fagan's whereabouts. They looked closely at every man they met, especially those with bushy whiskers or mustaches, or wearing farmer's big straw hats. The trio went up and down the less crowded lanes, but without success.

As they turned into a busier part of the fair, Billy paused at a weight-guessing booth. He lingered to watch while his companions walked on. The man who owned the booth was trying to calculate the weight of an enormously tall and heavy man. After a few steps Nan and Mr. Sheldon turned to wait for Billy.

At that moment a large woman pushed past Billy and, to their surprise, the boy fell heavily to the ground. The woman hurried on without turning and Nan saw, as she passed them, that she wore a huge hat and dark glasses.

They rushed to help Billy to his feet. "What a rude woman!" Nan exclaimed, "She didn't even stop to apologize!"

"Woman!" Billy cried. "That was no woman! I'm sure it was Ben Fagan, and he shoved me on purpose!"

With an exclamation Detective Sheldon was off, sprinting up the crowded walk as fast as he could. Nan and Billy ran after the detective, but before long they met him returning. He was mopping his perspiring face with his handkerchief.

"Fagan got away again," Tom Sheldon told them, with a shake of his head. "The fellow's slippery as an eel—dodged into one of the booths, I guess. I couldn't catch a glimpse of the woman with the big hat anywhere. At least I'm convinced Fagan's still in the vicinity. We'll have to keep closer watch on *everyone* we see."

"I believe I'd know his eyes," Nan said as they walked along, "if he didn't have on dark glasses." Suddenly she stopped.

"Oh," she breathed softly, "I have an idea! Let's go over to that bench. I don't want anyone to hear what I say."

When the trio had seated themselves, Nan told Billy and Detective Sheldon about her experience two days before in the ball-throwing booth. "I'm sure that someone was behind that curtain to keep the ball from going into the mouth, and that the eyes I saw were Mr. Fagan's. They made me feel creepy, just as his always do," Nan concluded excitedly.

"Is the man in charge of that booth quite short?" Billy asked.

"Yes," Nan answered. "I didn't like the way he acted, either."

Billy nodded. "He used to come to the merry-go-round late at night to see Ben Fagan. I think the two may have been up to something crooked."

The detective had followed this conversation

very closely. He slapped his knee joyfully. "I think you kids have the clue to this mystery. Now listen carefully."

The three of them conversed in whispers for a moment. Then they rose. Nan left Billy and the detective and went back to the dining tent. She found her mother and Aunt Sarah and the small twins waiting there.

"No luck so far," she reported. "I'll take Freddie and Flossie to throw some balls at the target until the others come back."

"Oh, goody!" cried Flossie, and Freddie added, "I was awfully tired of just sitting still!"

The women agreed, and Nan's mother said, "We'll stay right here. We'll see you at two-thirty."

Nan and the little twins set forth. They had to wait until a party of boys finished their ball-throwing contest. Then Nan bought five balls apiece for the twins and herself. Her heart was beating fast.

"You're first, Flossie," she said.

While Flossie was having her turn, Nan watched the eyes in the clown face. None of the balls struck the curtain, and the eyes appeared to be painted ones.

Freddie came next. Two of his missiles hit the

curtain but the third one went directly to the mouth and bounced back again. The fourth hit it and disappeared inside.

"Hooray, Nan!" he cried. "Now for the last one."

He fired his fifth ball which also went into the painted mouth. Nan was watching and laughing when suddenly there was a slight movement behind the curtain and, once again, a pair of human eyes looked straight at her.

Nan tried not to appear startled. She turned to Freddie and exclaimed, "Good! You're a fine shot! I'll try to equal you." She tied a large silk kerchief around her dark hair.

Nan's hand was trembling when she took up her first ball. She threw and it struck one of the cheeks on the clown face. The painted eyes were back in place.

"Hard luck, miss," jeered the squat concessionaire.

The next ball Nan aimed directly at one of the eyes. "There! If that old Ben Fagan is behind there he'll get whacked," she thought. The ball bounced off the left eye, which still looked painted.

As she poised for her third throw, Nan saw the painted eyes move to one side. The ones that replaced them were cold and staring. Without a

Nan threw the ball

doubt she knew they belonged to Ben Fagan. Frantically Nan wondered where Detective Sheldon could be.

Then all at once, before she could toss the ball, the eyes vanished and left blank holes in their place. The curtain swayed and bulged violently, and the sound of voices came from behind it. The man in charge went hastily back to investigate. Nan gasped in relief when she heard the detective say loudly:

"You've run up against the law this time, Fagan!"

Then two policemen came out from behind the curtain and started to close up the booth. One of them said to Nan, "This concession is out of business. The owner's under arrest."

Then Nan knew that her plan had been successful. She hurried the surprised Flossie and Freddie back to the dining tent and found the others there with her mother and Aunt Sarah. "It worked!" she called when she saw them. "My signal worked! They've got Ben Fagan and the man at the booth, and the police have closed the place."

"Wait a minute, Nan!" her father protested, laughing. "What's this all about?"

Her eyes sparkling with excitement, Nan told of her suspicions about the strange eyes at the ball-throwing booth, and how the tables had been turned on Fagan.

"What was your signal?" Freddie asked.

Nan touched the kerchief around her head. "This," she replied. "When I put on the kerchief, the police knew it was time to close in on Ben Fagan."

Just then Detective Sheldon and Billy arrived. The detective went straight to Nan and shook her hand. "Congratulations, young lady!" he exclaimed. "Your quick thinking did the trick. Ben Fagan has so many charges against him that he'll be in prison for a long time."

"And look, Bert!" Billy said with a grin, holding out a camera. "Fagan had it in his pocket when the police searched him!"

"Thanks a million, Billy," Bert exclaimed. "Now that mystery is solved, too."

"We've been watching Fagan for some time," the detective explained. "Ever since the fair opened there have been mysterious thefts. Now we have definite proof he's been responsible for them. He and the man who ran the target booth have been in league.

"Not only was that game as crooked as they come," he went on, "but Fagan had his own racket. He'd watch from behind the fake eyes in the clown face and when he saw a likely looking prospect, he'd sneak around in front and try to pick the man's pocket."

"Wow!" exclaimed Billy. "I never suspected that one!"

"Of course you didn't," the detective said. "Neither did Mr. Bates. Fagan was a clever man, but his own greed led to his capture. Fagan couldn't resist a dollar—not even an honest one," he laughed. "That's why he risked staying here and disguised himself to take the waiter's job."

"Oh, what a wicked man!" exclaimed Aunt Sarah. "He certainly deserves to be punished and most of all for his mistreatment of Billy."

"I'm certainly glad he's been caught," said Mr. Bobbsey. "No telling what a man like that might do next."

"Thanks to you Bobbseys and Billy here," commented Detective Sheldon, "he's going to have a long time to think about his wrongdoings."

"And who would have thought we'd have so much excitement at the Bolton County Fair!" Nan exclaimed as they waved good-by to the detective.

"As Harry says," Uncle Daniel laughed, "there's always some adventure when you Bobbseys come to Meadowbrook."

"I can believe that, Dan," said Mr. Gardner.

Then he added, "Do you mind if Billy drives back with me? I have something to discuss with him."

Uncle Daniel nodded. "That will be fine, John. We'll see you at Meadowbrook."

The Bobbseys were in front of the farmhouse when Mr. Gardner pulled into the driveway. He and Billy got out. They were both smiling broadly.

"You'll all be glad to know that Billy has consented to stay with Mrs. Gardner and me," the lawyer said. "And if he grows to like us as much as we like him, we hope to adopt him as our son."

"Whoopee!" Harry shouted. "We'll be neighbors!"

"And we can see you whenever we come to Meadowbrook!" cried Bert.

"And you'll have calliope music, too," Billy said joyfully. "Mr. Gardner is going to buy it from Mr. Bates." Then he looked serious. "I wish there was something I could do for you Bobbseys," he remarked. "It's because of all you've done that I'm going to have a real family and a home."

Bert looked thoughtful. "Billy," he said, "I'd almost forgotten about it, but were you near the bus just before it rolled down into the lake at the school picnic?"

Billy hung his head. "Yes, I was," he acknowledged. "And I heard you and that other boy talking, and I saw him release the brake. I shouldn't have run away, but I was afraid Ben Fagan would beat me if I didn't get right back."

Bert quickly reassured him, saying, "I don't blame you. But would you be willing to write our principal, Mr. Tetlow, and tell him what you heard and saw? It would make me feel a lot better!"

"Of course I will, Bert," Billy promised. "Whizzikers! I didn't know you had been accused of it."

"That makes everything just about perfect," Nan said blissfully.

"Yes," Freddie spoke up. "Only I hope we have another adventure soon."

"Oh, we will," Flossie said, and everyone laughingly agreed.

At that moment the twins' mother and Aunt Sarah came from the house with trays of lemonade and cookies which they set down on the table under the tree.

Billy took his glass and jumped up on a chair, crying, "Here's to the Bobbsey twins and all their family!"

"And here's to the county fair!" chorused the twins.